"I know I said I never wanted a family, but that was before Lexi existed. She's my daughter and she's a Devilliers."

Icicles pierced Mia's heart. "So what are you saying?"

"I'm telling you now that I won't expect anything less than full access to my daughter, and the most expedient and practical way for that to happen is for us to marry."

Daniel was surprised at how easily those words had tripped off his tongue. He hadn't even consciously decided *what* the best solution was, but something about Mia's proximity and the tangled emotions she was evoking, not to mention the memories, had prompted him to say what he had.

And now he found that he couldn't even drum up much regret or even shock at his words. But he could see shock on Mia's face.

Suddenly her face blanked. It was as if she was aware she was giving too much away and had learned to hide behind a bland mask. It irritated Daniel intensely.

She was pale. She shook her head. "No way."

Irish author **Abby Green** ended a very glamorous career in film and TV—which really consisted of a lot of standing in the rain outside actors' trailers—to pursue her love of romance. After she'd bombarded Harlequin with manuscripts, they kindly accepted one, and an author was born. She lives in Dublin, Ireland, and loves any excuse for distraction. Visit abby-green.com or email abbygreenauthor@gmail.com.

Books by Abby Green

Harlequin Presents

The Greek's Unknown Bride

Hot Summer Nights with a Billionaire

The Flaw in His Red-Hot Revenge

One Night With Consequences

An Innocent, A Seduction, A Secret

The Marchetti Dynasty

The Maid's Best Kept Secret
The Innocent Behind the Scandal
Bride Behind the Desert Veil

Rival Spanish Brothers

Confessions of a Pregnant Cinderella
Redeemed by His Stolen Bride

Visit the Author Profile page at Harlequin.com for more titles.

Abby Green

BOUND BY HER SHOCKING SECRET

Recycling programs for this product may not exist in your area.

ISBN-13: 978-1-335-56814-4

Bound by Her Shocking Secret

Copyright © 2021 by Abby Green

This edition published by arrangement with Harlequin Books S.A.

For questions and comments about the quality of this book, please contact us at CustomerService@Harlequin.com.

Harlequin Enterprises ULC
22 Adelaide St. West, 40th Floor
Toronto, Ontario M5H 4E3, Canada
www.Harlequin.com

Printed in U.S.A.

BOUND BY HER
SHOCKING SECRET

CHAPTER ONE

DANIEL DEVILLIERS SURVEYED the scene below him, where guests thronged the main *salon* floor. The iconic Devilliers jewellers, which had been standing at this location on Place Vendôme, one of Paris's most exclusive addresses, since the eighteenth century, had been totally updated and refurbished in the last six months and this evening was the grand reopening.

Since his father's death a few years ago, when Daniel had inherited one of the most enduring brands in the world, he'd slowly but surely been working with a very conservative and resistant board to haul Devilliers into the twenty-first century. And his efforts were finally paying off.

It was a triumph. The party of the month. The year. Invitations had been sought after by heads of state and royalty. But Daniel was eager to open up Devilliers to a more varied and vibrant demographic, and more than a few VIPs had been reduced to begging for admission.

Actors and actresses rubbed shoulders with politicians and titans of industry, and amongst them moved the most beautiful models in the world, male and female, showcasing the brand's latest and legacy designs, from a new cutting edge wristwatch design to a diamond tiara that had been made for Empress Josephine.

Diamonds, rubies, pearls, sapphires and emeralds, set amongst gold, platinum and silver, sparkled and vied for attention on the models, complemented by dresses specially chosen to display the jewellery to best advantage.

Vintage champagne flowed freely and guests were offered hors d'oeuvres that resembled small pieces of sculpture, yet still eminently edible and delicious.

Framed black and white photos adorned the walls, depicting the history of Devilliers. An oil painting of the wife of the man who had founded the company hung in pride of place on a central wall, her intricate tiara sparkling amongst the elaborate up-do of her thick dark brown hair. Distinctive grey eyes looked out from a haughtily beautiful face. The same eyes and aristocratic features that had made it down through the generations to Daniel.

Except in Daniel those aristocratic features were hewn into something far more masculine and uncompromising. High cheekbones and a surprisingly sensual mouth were countered by deep-set eyes and a hard jaw. Together with thick dark hair cut short, and his tall, powerfully lean build, the whole package of an Alpha male in his prime was a siren call to anyone with a pulse.

A movement caught Daniel's eye, and he saw his PR advisor motioning for him to come down. He knew he should join the party. But he'd taken a moment out to observe, to feel... He wasn't sure what he'd been hoping to feel. A sense of triumph that his vision was finally being realised? A sense of satisfaction? But he didn't feel either of those things. What he did feel was a certain kind of anti-climax. A flatness.

And then something else caught his eye. A strapless black satin dress. A flash of tawny-gold hair, piled high. The smooth slope of bare shoulders, lightly golden. His insides clenched in helpless reaction before he could control his response.

Whoever it was had disappeared behind a column. Out of sight. It had only been a flicker of recognition. It wouldn't have been her. She wouldn't have the nerve to appear on his turf again. *It couldn't have been her.* And yet Daniel's pulse was hammering under his skin at the very notion.

Memories, vivid and provocative, clawed at the edges of his mind, seeking purchase. A laughing face, bright white teeth. Lush mouth. Sparkling light green eyes. Wild tawny hair wrapped around his hand as he thrust deeper and deeper into an embrace so hot and tight he'd never wanted to stop.

And other memories, less carnal. A pale face, huge eyes red-rimmed from tears. Pain. A block of ice in his chest, freezing the blood in his veins.

'It's probably for the best. We both know this.'

'Get out, Daniel. I don't ever want to see you again.'

Daniel shook his head to dislodge the very unwelcome memories. The present returned. The chatter from the level beneath him. The music from the string quartet he'd had flown in from Vienna.

Angry with himself for indulging in this moment, Daniel pushed back from the railing that bordered the mezzanine area and moved to go downstairs. The past was the past and it had no place here. The future beckoned, and as Daniel came down the wide spiral staircase he pushed every lingering wisp of memories of *her* down so deep that they would be crushed for ever.

He caught the eye of one stunningly beautiful woman at the bottom of the stairs. She smiled and it was explicit. It didn't move him in the slightest. *Perfect*.

Mia Forde knew she couldn't hide in the toilet cubicle all night. She cursed herself. How on earth had she thought it would be a good idea to confront Daniel again at the relaunch party for the iconic Devilliers *salon*?

She knew why and she felt pathetic now. She'd thought that by being in a public setting it wouldn't be so daunting. And also, weakly, she'd thought that wearing the full armour of designer clothes and make-up would make it easier to stand in front of Daniel again.

Even though, when they'd been together, their relationship had never been about that. Their relationship had been the antithesis of this sleek, rarefied world. She'd never appeared in public with Daniel in an official capacity. Not like his other lovers. She hadn't wanted to. For lots of reasons that she didn't have time to dwell on now.

A security guard was waiting outside, tasked with guarding the stunning yellow topaz and diamond necklace and matching earrings she was wearing as she had managed to get herself hired as one of the models to showcase Devilliers jewels for the evening.

She took a breath and left the cubicle, went back into the main part of the bathroom which was mercifully empty. She caught a glimpse of her reflection and grimaced. Her eyes looked too big and scared. The lipstick that had been applied earlier was all but bitten off her mouth. Her cheeks were still pink after catching her first glimpse of Daniel, where he'd been standing on the upper level, those cool grey eyes surveying the scene.

She hadn't been able to breathe at that first sight of him, paralysed by the onslaught of so many things— memories, emotions, anger… But worst of all the return of a physical awareness so acute and visceral that it had been like a punch in the gut.

His eyeline had turned towards where she'd stood and somehow she'd managed to make her shocked limbs move, tucking out of sight before he could see her.

And now here she was, trembling like a leaf. Which was pathetic when she considered what she'd been through in the past two years. She'd become stronger than she'd ever been. Fierce, even. She could handle seeing Daniel Devilliers again. She was just here to impart a message and then she would leave, head held high.

The jewels glittered against her skin, set off beautifully thanks to the simplicity of the black satin dress. She looked at them dispassionately. Worth many thousands of euros. And yet they left her cold. Because she knew they were just pretty stones. Dead inside. Like her relationship had been with Daniel. Oh, there had been heat and fire. She felt weak at the thought of it. But no heart. No soul. No depth.

In fact, the man couldn't be more perfectly suited to his inherited profession. All fire and heat on the surface but cold inside.

And was that his fault? a voice asked.

Mia sighed. No, it wasn't his fault. He'd never made her any promises because she'd explicitly told him that their relationship was just about the physical and the transitory. She'd put up so many walls to guard her heart against him that when they'd crumbled it had all been too late. There had been no relationship to save.

At that moment Mia heard approaching voices and straightened her shoulders. She had to go and find him now. The door opened and a couple of women came in with a flurry of overpowering perfume. Mia avoided their eyes but couldn't fail to hear their conversation.

'Did you see him standing up there? Like some kind of god?'

'I've never seen anyone so sexy in my life...'

'He's divorced now...it was all over the papers. Single again...'

A sharp pain lanced Mia when she heard those words: *divorced...single again.* She forced the pain and sting of jealousy down. They had no place here.

She was almost at the door when her clutch bag vibrated. It could only be one person. She pulled out her phone and immediately her forehead creased in worry.

The other two women were in cubicles now, still continuing their indiscreet conversation.

Mia quickly made a call. 'What's wrong, Simone? Is everything okay?'

Her friend spoke on the other end and Mia's blood ran cold. She forgot everything and had one primal response. *She had to get home now.*

She said, 'Don't worry, I'll be right there.'

Terminating the call, she put her phone back in her clutch and left the bathroom, all thoughts of Daniel Devilliers eclipsed.

Daniel was doing the social rounds in the belly of the party. He could see a long line of people waiting to speak with him and swallowed a sigh of frustration. And then he berated himself. This evening was the first glittering milestone in achieving all he wanted to achieve with Devilliers. So why couldn't he just damn enjoy it?

But the frustration prickling under his skin wouldn't go away. Taunting him. A small voice in his head said: *If you're not satisfied with this then when will you ever feel satisfied?*

It irritated him intensely, because he'd never been under any illusions that his loyalty to his inheritance was born out of sentimental emotion. The opposite, in fact. He'd always viewed it with a very dispassionate discerning eye. Any loyalty he did feel came from a sense of responsibility to the hundreds of workers behind this legacy, some of whom had worked for Devilliers over generations, and his own personal ambition to see the brand evolve and become an even bigger success.

You're doing this for your sister too, a small voice reminded him.

A familiar tightness made Daniel absently touch his

chest. Yes, if there was any sentiment attached it was for his sister, who had loved coming to the *salon* as a child, staring in awe at all the sparkling gems, asking reverently, 'Do we really own all of these?'

Daniel pushed the past aside. He found that his gaze was wandering, looking for a glimpse of tawny gold hair.

It hadn't been her. Let it go.

Angry with himself for dwelling on a ghost from his past, he reminded himself that there were plenty of beautiful, willing women in his immediate vicinity. Not ghosts. And he didn't need the reminder of how long it had been since he'd had a lover in his bed.

Not since her.

One was approaching him now. Blonde. Icy cool in a white dress. Blue eyes. Her throat, arms and ears literally dripped with diamonds. She was smiling with the kind of sexual confidence mixed with avarice that Daniel knew all too well. He told himself this was exactly what he was looking for, even as something inside him recoiled when she came closer.

But just before she could reach him someone else approached from the side. One of his security detail, who said, close to his ear, 'Sorry to bother you, sir, but there's been an incident.'

Daniel looked at him, the approaching woman forgotten. 'Incident?'

'A woman—one of the models—was trying to leave with her jewellery.'

Daniel raised a brow. 'If she's been apprehended why do I need to be involved?'

The man looked uncomfortable. 'She's saying she knows you and that you can vouch for her.'

A prickling sensation tickled the back of Daniel's neck. He asked, 'Where is she?'

'In the security office.'

Emitting a sound of irritation, Daniel strode towards the front of the *salon*. The security office was near the main entrance, its door camouflaged to look like a mirrored wall. Another security guard was waiting there for him, looking grim.

'Sorry to disturb you, sir. She's in here.'

The man opened the door into a large room with its walls covered in screens showing every inch of the *salon* and all the other rooms.

It took a second for Daniel's eyes to adjust to the dim bluish light so he didn't see her at first, standing in the centre of the room.

But then he did. And for a heart-stopping moment he thought he might be hallucinating. But then he forced oxygen to his lungs and brain. *She wasn't a ghost.* He hadn't imagined seeing her earlier.

Mia Forde. The last woman he'd ever expected to see again. The last woman he'd wanted to see ever again.

And yet even as he told himself that he couldn't stop or deny the helpless physical reaction heating his blood and making his body tight. Forcing him to exert control.

She looked as beautiful as he remembered. More so. After two years. She'd been twenty-one when they'd met. Now it was as if a layer had been removed to reveal the woman underneath. Her face seemed more... angular. Cheekbones more defined. That lush, wide mouth was as provocative as ever, even when pursed in a line of tension.

It was only then that Daniel noted the black satin gown. Strapless. Hugging her curves. The top of the dress couldn't hide the swells of her breasts. He could still see them in his mind's eye, full and high. Her tempting nipples—

Daniel slammed down on that incendiary memory. The knowledge that this woman still had the ability to short-circuit his rational brain was like pouring acid onto an old wound.

It made his voice curt. 'What the hell are you doing here, Mia?'

Mia had to lock her legs to stay upright, when every instinct was telling her to curl up, hide. *Run.*

The expressions crossing Daniel's face might have been comical if Mia had felt remotely like laughing. There had been recognition, shock, disbelief, and now blistering anger.

Fatally, she couldn't take her eyes off his lean face, even as she said faintly to the security guard who had hauled her in here, 'See? I told you I knew him.'

Daniel folded his arms, which made his biceps bulge against the fabric of his tuxedo. 'What are you doing here? Is this some kind of sick joke?'

Mia recovered some of her wits. 'A joke? Do you really think I set out to be here this evening just for a few lols because I've nothing better to do on a Saturday night?'

The fact that her usual Saturday night routine was dinner, maybe a TV movie and then faceplanting into bed before ten p.m. was not something she was about to divulge in this hostile atmosphere.

His eye dropped to where the necklace and earrings she'd been wearing were laid out on the table beside where she stood. 'Were you really trying to steal the jewels?'

'Of course not. I just… I got a call. I panicked. I forgot I was wearing them. I'm not a thief.'

Daniel frowned. 'How did you even get in here?'

Hurt lanced Mia. 'I was hired to work here this evening. I know we share a…a complicated history, but I wasn't aware that I was on some persona non grata list.'

Now Daniel looked frustrated. He unfolded his arms and slashed a hand through the air. 'I don't mean like that. I just mean…' He stopped. And then, 'Why would you come here?'

'I needed to talk to you. When my agent arranged for me to be one of your models I figured it would be an easier way to…to get to you.'

A man as famous and wealthy as Daniel Devilliers was nigh on impossible to contact unless he wanted you to contact him. As Mia had found out to her cost when she'd discovered that the number she had for him was no longer in use.

But the panic that had galvanised her to leave in the first place, before she'd even spoken to him, surged up again. She said, 'Look, I really do have to go. It's an emergency. Can I leave, please?'

Much to Daniel's chagrin, his first reaction to Mia saying she wanted to leave wasn't abject relief. It was a tangled mess of many things, including a resurgence of desire that was as powerful as it was unwelcome.

'You said you needed to talk to me. What about?'

He noticed now that Mia looked pale beneath her natural all-American tan. 'I can't explain now. I just have to go.'

'You were caught in the act of leaving while wearing hundreds of thousands of euros worth of jewels. You owe me an explanation.'

Mia was wringing her hands in front of her. 'I know. Look, I wasn't thinking. I forgot I had them on. You *know* me. You know I'd never steal anything!'

A memory assailed Daniel before he could stop it. He'd opened a velvet box and Mia had looked down, her eyes widening with predictable awe, as she'd taken in the stunning pearl bracelet with a diamond-studded flower in the centre. She'd even touched it reverently, saying, 'It's beautiful.'

Daniel had said idly, 'One of our new designs.'

Then she'd looked at him with genuine confusion. 'What is this?'

'A gift.'

She'd shaken her head. 'But…this isn't that kind of relationship.'

Daniel could remember feeling a sense of frustration that she wasn't behaving as he expected. As he was used to. Even though, at every step of the way since he'd first asked her out, she'd behaved contrary to any other woman he'd ever known. At first she'd told him it would be one date. Then, when they'd slept together, that it would be one night. But one date and one night had bled into more dates, and more nights, because the chemistry had been just too strong to ignore.

Even then, she'd always made a point of making sure he knew that she didn't expect more. In many ways it should have been Daniel's dream scenario: a woman who set out boundaries before he even had to. Because he certainly didn't want more either. But some rogue part of him had been prompted at that moment to ask, 'What kind of relationship is this, Mia?'

'Not one where you give me...stuff.'

He'd felt bemused. 'Do you have any idea what this *stuff* is worth?'

She'd backed away then. 'I don't care, Daniel. It's lovely...truly. But I don't want it. I'd feel uncomfortable.'

It had been the first time a woman had refused a gift from him. Daniel might have cynically suspected it was some kind of ploy, in spite of Mia's protestations, but the following morning when he'd been leaving her apartment she'd handed him the box saying, 'Don't forget this.'

'You really don't want it?'

'Thank you, but no.'

The past faded. The present returned. Mia said with a desperate tone in her voice, 'Please, Daniel, I need to go.'

'If it was anyone else we'd be calling the police.'

Now she went so pale Daniel thought she might faint. He even reached out, but she backed away, her hip bumping awkwardly on the corner of the table.

'Mia, dammit... Why are you here?'

She bit her lip and Daniel had to curl his hand into a fist to stop himself from reaching out to tug that lower lip free. It had been one of her habits before, which he'd suspected she'd played on because she knew it drove him crazy.

She spoke so fast he almost didn't hear her.

'It's my daughter. I have to get home to her. My friend is babysitting and Lexi has a high temperature and she's vomiting.'

Daniel went cold inside. 'You have a baby?'

It had been two years. Of course she could have had a baby by now. *Another baby*. With someone else. *Lexi. A girl*.

'Yes.'

Daniel shook his head, words coming out before he had time to rationalise why he needed to know. 'How? Who…?'

Mia looked at him. The moment stretched.

Daniel became aware of the silent presence of at least two guards, who had been watching this interplay. He said abruptly, without looking at them, 'Please leave us.'

The guards left.

Mia looked at him.

His sense of the ground beneath him shifting slightly was disconcerting. There was no need to think at all that this child could be—

Mia said, 'I really don't want to get into this now. I have to go to her.'

But something dark compelled Daniel to say, 'I'll let you go when you tell me who her father is. Are you still with him?'

Mia swallowed. Her heart was beating like a trapped bird in her chest. She'd hoped against hope that Daniel would have lost his appeal since she'd seen him last, that any desire had been incinerated by the words he'd said to her before he'd walked out.

'I think this is for the best.'

But no. Her body was still attuned to his as if it was an instrument that sang only in proximity to him. And when she thought of the amazing things her body had done since she'd seen him last it was even more galling.

She'd had a baby. She'd experienced one of the most primal, beautiful things on earth. And yet right now all she could think of was the fact that Daniel looked even leaner and more powerful than the last time she'd seen him.

He'd never had any softness, but it was as if a layer had been removed to reveal the starkness of the man underneath. All edges and angles and hard muscles. Unforgiving.

'It's for the best.'

She tried to stay focused. Her main priority was getting out of here ASAP. 'No, I'm not with the father.'

'Who is he?'

Mia's heart stopped and then started again. She longed to be able to say, *You don't know him* or, *It's none of your business.* But she couldn't lie and she couldn't prevaricate.

This was why she had come here after all.

She took a deep breath but still felt breathless.

'Mia—'

'She's yours.'

They spoke at the same time. Daniel's mouth shut.

His expression went blank. She wasn't sure if he'd heard.

Mia said, 'She's your daughter. Eighteen months.'

It wasn't often that a man like Daniel Devilliers was left lost for words—not that Mia could enjoy the novel experience right now.

'Look, I'm sorry… That's why I came this evening. I was hoping to get a chance to arrange a meeting with you. I didn't want to tell you like…this.'

In the security office of the Devilliers *salon*, with every important and famous person in France just feet away, having been accused of trying to steal Devilliers jewels.

Eventually Daniel spoke. 'But…how?'

Mia's phone started to vibrate inside her bag, which was on the table. She reached for it, seeing her friend's name. She answered and listened for a second and then said, 'Okay, look… I'm leaving now. I'll be there as soon as I can.'

She terminated the phone call and looked at Daniel. 'I'm very sorry to have had to tell you like this, but I have to go *now.*'

She spied a pen and paper on the table and scribbled down her address and phone number. 'If you are going to insist on calling the police, or whatever, or when you're ready to talk, this is where I live now.'

She handed the piece of paper to Daniel, who took it, still looking shocked.

Mia took her bag and walked to the door. She opened it and went out, but a security guard held up his hand.

He looked over her shoulder, presumably at Daniel. 'Sir...?'

There was nothing from behind her, and Mia was close to shoving the security guard out of the way, but then she heard Daniel's deep voice.

'Let her go.'

Relief flooded her system. She vaguely heard Daniel say something else, but she was already at the entrance of the *salon*, where a bank of paparazzi were waiting. She saw them lift their cameras and then lower them again. She wasn't recognisable to them. She might have been a model, but she'd never attained supermodel status. And when she'd gone out with Daniel they'd managed to evade the glare of publicity.

But Mia couldn't care less about not being recognised. What was far worse was that she couldn't see any taxis waiting. Feeling panic rise, she was about to take out her phone to try and use a taxi app when her arm was taken by a big hand. A familiar touch.

Daniel.

She looked up. 'What...?'

He was grim. Not looking at her, tugging her back towards the *salon* before the photographers noticed. 'Come on, I'll take you home. My car is at the side entrance.'

Mia was so relieved that she would shortly be in a vehicle heading to her baby that she just followed Daniel along a corridor that led to another entrance.

A sleek black car was waiting in the street. The driver was standing by an open back door. Daniel handed the driver the piece of paper with Mia's address on it and helped her into the car before getting in on the other side.

Then they were moving. It was only as they left Place Vendôme behind that Mia realised what was happening. Daniel was coming with her. A different kind of panic gripped her. She wasn't ready for him to meet Lexi yet. To explain everything.

She looked at him in the gloom of the back of the car. His profile was stern. As she watched, he tugged at the bowtie at his throat, undoing it, flicking open a button on his shirt with long, dextrous fingers. His hands were masculine. She remembered being surprised that they weren't soft, as she might have expected of a businessman…of a billionaire who handled precious gems every day.

To Mia's disgust, flames of desire burst to life in her belly at that memory.

'You shouldn't have left the party. It's an important night,' she said.

He looked at her and her skin prickled with heat.

'Yes, it is. But the news that apparently I'm a father has managed to eclipse the importance of the evening.'

The driver put up the privacy partition. Mia knew Daniel. She had been subjected to his very persuasive and determined brand of seduction, so she knew it would be nigh on impossible to persuade him to change his course of action.

Nevertheless, she tried. 'It's really not appropriate to come with me now. Lexi might be—'

'Lexi. What kind of name is that?'

Mia bristled defensively. 'It's short for Alexandra.'

'You say it's not appropriate for me to come with

you now? Yet you thought it was "appropriate" to come and disrupt one of the most important nights in the Devilliers calendar?'

Mia refused to feel as if she was in the wrong. 'If I had been able to contact you through regular channels then obviously I would have done that. And I did try. But the number I have for you is no longer in operation, and when I tried to contact you through your office they refused to pass on just my name. I had to give more detail, and I wasn't prepared to tell a stranger what I had to tell you. I would have come to the *salon*, but as it was being renovated, obviously you weren't in the office there.'

'We set up temporary headquarters nearby.'

'It would have been easier to try and arrange a meeting with the President of the United States.'

Daniel wasn't amused. 'If what you say is true and this…this baby is mine—which I can't understand is possible since I saw you after—'

Mia cut him off before he could say it. 'She's yours.'

Daniel's jaw clenched. 'If she is, then why didn't you come to me before now?'

A familiar ball of pain that Mia hated to acknowledge lodged in her gut, dousing the flames of desire. 'You were married.'

A muscle in Daniel's jaw ticked. 'Nevertheless, I deserved to know.'

'As soon as I read about your divorce I started trying to contact you.'

'What if I hadn't divorced?'

The ball of pain got heavier as she considered that. In truth, Mia hadn't really contemplated the long-term plan, and that made her defensive. 'If you hadn't divorced, I would have told you at some stage.'

Daniel made a disbelieving sound.

Before Mia could lose her nerve, she said, 'I'm sorry, by the way. About the divorce. No matter what the circumstances of your marriage were, I can't imagine it was easy.'

'By "circumstances" you mean the fact that it was an arranged marriage?'

Mia and Daniel had been dating for almost two months when a headline had appeared in the newspapers, speculating about a long-standing arrangement for Daniel to marry an heiress from one of France's other great dynastic families. The news that he was promised to someone in marriage had blindsided her, reminding her painfully of a similar experience at the hands of her first boyfriend.

When she'd confronted Daniel about it, he'd been dismissive. 'It's not an *engagement*. It's an ancient agreement that was arranged by my grandfather when he had to borrow money from the Valois family. To be honest, I'd forgotten about it.'

Mia had replied angrily. 'Well, it seems your intended fiancée hasn't forgotten.'

She'd thrown the paper down on the floor between them in her apartment, leaving the luminously pretty face of his future wife, dark-eyed and dark-haired, staring up at them impassively.

And at that moment Mia had suddenly thought of something. 'No wonder you were so happy to go under the radar with our affair—because you knew this was imminent and you didn't want our relationship to appear in the press right now.'

He'd looked at her, his dark grey gaze narrowing. 'You were the one who dictated the terms of this affair. You specifically said you didn't expect any commitment, that you were happy to keep things casual, discreet.'

She had. And it had hit her in that moment that, in spite of her best efforts to protect herself from developing any feelings beyond the physical for this man, she'd failed woefully.

A prickling sense of shame and exposure had made her realise how badly she'd exposed herself. She'd vowed never to fall for a man like Daniel again—rich and privileged—and yet there she was, her heart feeling as if it had been sliced open.

Mia's attention came back to the present moment when she noticed the car was turning into her quiet street. Daniel had been right that day. She hadn't wanted anything more. But somewhere along the way she'd forgotten the lessons of her past and had humiliated herself spectacularly.

The car pulled to a stop outside the tall building where she had an apartment on the top floor. She looked at Daniel. 'I really would prefer if we could arrange another time to meet.'

He looked at her. 'Tough. I deserve answers, and I'm not going anywhere until I get them.'

CHAPTER TWO

AT MIA'S FRONT door she stopped and turned to face Daniel, who was behind her, taking up an inordinate amount of space in the small landing. 'Can you just give me a minute? I need to make sure Lexi is okay and if she sees you she might get upset… She's not used to men being in the apartment.'

Mia hated admitting that, but there were more important considerations right now.

She could see the struggle on Daniel's face. Eventually he said, 'Five minutes, Mia.'

Mia turned back and opened the door and slipped inside. Simone appeared in the doorway to the bedroom, holding a flushed-looking Lexi. Mia's heart clenched. She was a mini carbon copy of the man outside the door. Dark curly hair framed a cherubic face and huge grey eyes. But, as Mia was discovering lately, the cherubic exterior could change in a heartbeat to something far less angelic!

'Mama!' Lexi held out her arms and Mia scooped her into her chest, murmuring words of comfort while assessing her.

Her friend Simone said, 'I'm so sorry, Mia, I probably overreacted. But I've never seen a baby get sick before and it scared the life out of me.'

Mia sent her a wry smile. 'Honestly, it's way better to overreact than do nothing. This little one has given me quite a few scares along the way.'

Mia took Lexi into the bathroom and checked her temperature. A couple of minutes later she let out another sigh of relief. 'Normal.'

Her friend grinned and chucked Lexi under the chin, making her giggle. 'You little fiend—you had me all wound up!'

Aware that Daniel was undoubtedly pacing up and down outside her front door, Mia said, 'Look, thanks, Simone. You should try and make something of your evening while you can.'

Her friend looked at her. 'You could go back to the party if you want?'

There was a peremptory knock on the door. Her friend frowned. Mia shook her head. 'I don't need to go back.'

Mia walked to the door with her, Lexi a sleepy weight in her arms. Her friend gathered her bag and coat and looked at her with a mischievous expression. 'Did you bring the party home?'

Mia smiled weakly at the thought of Daniel's grim face. 'Not quite.'

She opened the door and could see Simone's eyes widen as she took in the vision of an impatient Daniel Devilliers being made to wait.

Ever the gentleman, though, he greeted her friend. 'Good evening.'

Mia remembered her manners. 'Simone, this is

Daniel Devilliers. Simone is an old friend of mine. She was kind enough to babysit this evening.'

Her friend was uncharacteristically silent. When Mia looked at her she was staring at Daniel as if she'd never seen a man before, and then she looked at Lexi. And then at Mia, who said hurriedly, 'Thanks again for tonight.'

Simone left.

Alone again, Mia sucked in a breath and steeled herself to deal with Daniel—only to find him staring at Lexi with such an arrested expression on his face that she immediately felt concern.

'What is it?'

She looked down at Lexi to check her, but she seemed fine. Her colour had gone back to normal. She had her thumb in her mouth and she was just looking at Daniel.

Mia looked at him again and could see that he was pale. Did he see the marked resemblance?

A little nervously she asked, 'Are you okay? You look like you've seen a ghost.'

Daniel didn't even hear what Mia was saying. All he could see was his sister's face. Right in front of him. The same black curly hair. Huge eyes. Rosebud mouth. Plump cheeks. She'd used to reach out her pudgy arms and call him to lift her up. *'Danny... Danny.'* Even when she could say Daniel, she'd used to keep calling him Danny.

He could still hear the panicked shriek of his name as if it was yesterday, and then the splash of water...

'Daniel... *Daniel?*'

The past receded and he saw Mia was looking at him. He felt exposed.

She stepped back. 'Please, come in.'

Mia went into the small apartment and he followed her. High ceilings gave it a sense of space. It was un- cluttered. Simple. Comfortable furniture demonstrated Mia's good eye for classic pieces. He remembered that from her old apartment. How he'd found it soothing.

Lexi's face appeared over Mia's shoulder as she twisted to look at Daniel. She took her thumb out of her mouth and declared, 'Man!'

Mia turned around to face Daniel. The sight of his ex-lover in a full-length evening gown holding a child—*his child*—was almost incomprehensible.

'What happened just then?' Mia asked.

Reluctantly Daniel said, 'She reminded me of some- one.'

'Who?'

Even more reluctantly, Daniel said, 'My sister.'

Mia frowned. 'You never mentioned you had a sis- ter.'

A solid weight lodged in Daniel's chest. 'She's dead.'

'Oh… I'm sorry.'

'It was a long time ago.'

'But Lexi reminds you of her?'

Daniel couldn't help nodding, looking at the child again. It was too huge to think of her as *his*. As his daughter. 'They could have been twins.'

Mia made a small sound and Daniel's gaze moved to her. She'd gone pale again.

Before he could wonder about her reaction she

shifted the baby in her arms and said, 'I need to change her, give her a bottle and put her down—then we can talk. Help yourself to a drink, or there's a coffee machine in the kitchen.' She turned, but then stopped, looked back. 'That is if you still drink coffee like you used to…'

Another memory blasted Daniel. Mia shaking her head and saying, *'Honestly, you drink too much of that stuff—it's no wonder you can't sleep.'*

She'd taken the coffee cup out of his hand to come and straddle his lap, pushing aside his laptop on which he'd been looking at a document. He'd looked up at her, at the wild tumble of her tawny hair over her shoulders. She'd been wearing only his shirt, haphazardly buttoned, the luscious curve of her breasts clearly visible.

He'd put his hands on her waist. No underwear. His hands had explored the smooth roundness of her buttocks, finding the centre of her exposed body, making her squirm against him as his mouth had fastened on one taut nipple and—

'…back in a few minutes…'

Daniel blinked. Mia was disappearing into another room, presumably a bedroom. The door closed behind her. He took a deep breath and ran a hand through his hair, still reeling from the vividness of the memory and the fact that there was no doubt in his mind that the child she'd held in her arms just now was his. His daughter.

So all that left was the burning question of how on earth it could be possible.

Daniel spied the drinks trolley in a corner of the room and went over, finding an unopened bottle of whisky and a tumbler. He poured himself a generous shot and swallowed it in one gulp, the fire racing down his throat doing little to make him feel any calmer.

Mia looked down at a sleeping Lexi for a long minute, knowing it was futile to delay the inevitable any longer. Daniel had been waiting for half an hour now—she could only imagine how irritated he would be. He'd never been good at waiting for other people, having little tolerance of those who couldn't keep up with his demanding pace.

But babies adhered to their own schedule, and it had taken some time to put Lexi down after the distraction of Simone babysitting her and then the strange man. But Mia was certain that she was okay now, and that was the main thing.

Mia stepped away from the cot and realised she was still wearing the evening dress. It felt too constrictive now. Too revealing. She quickly pulled down the side zip and tugged the dress down and off, finding a pair of worn jeans and a long-sleeved shirt, doing up the buttons hurriedly.

She tugged at her hair, pulling it down from the elaborate up-do, knowing it would look unkempt and wild, but it made her feel more herself.

She took a breath and opened the door, and saw Daniel immediately. Impossible not to in the small space which seemed even smaller now. He was sitting on her two-seater couch, dwarfing it to Lilliputian proportions. He'd taken off his jacket and his bowtie was hanging loose. One arm was stretched carelessly across the back of the couch and one ankle rested on the knee of his other leg.

He looked relaxed, but Mia could feel the tension. He had a glass resting on his bent knee, the golden liquid at the bottom catching the light.

He lifted the glass towards her. 'I hope you don't mind? I had to open the bottle.'

She shook her head. 'No, of course not.'

Her throat felt dry. She went and sat on the edge of the armchair that faced the couch, feeling like a guest in her own apartment. Part of her longed for a drink too, to give her some sense of confidence, but she also needed her wits about her. Daniel Devilliers had an ability to make her forget...*everything*.

'So, are you going to explain to me how it's possible that I have a child—a daughter—when the last time I saw you was in hospital, after you'd miscarried the baby?'

Mia was clasping her hands so tight she wasn't aware of her knuckles showing white. The memory of Daniel standing at the foot of her bed, pale and grim, was still too vivid. And those words.

'It's probably for the best.'

She shook her head, as if that could rearrange her thoughts into some sort of coherency.

'Mia, you owe me an explanation.'

She looked at Daniel and realised that he must have thought she didn't intend telling him. She stood up, agitated. Too many memories were crowding out the present moment.

'I know. I just... Give me a second, okay?'

She went over to the window that looked out over

the rooftops of the Parisian buildings nearby. Always one of her favourite views. She could see other people moving around their apartments. She could also feel Daniel's gaze, boring between her shoulderblades.

She turned around, arms folded. Before she could speak, though, she saw Daniel's gaze drop to her chest. Something flashed in his eyes. Something that was all too memorable and that precipitated an answering flash of heat in her solar plexus. She looked down to see that she'd done the buttons of her shirt up wrongly and there was a clear view of her ample cleavage through the gap above her folded arms.

She cursed and quickly uncrossed her arms, fingers fumbling to straighten the buttons. Embarrassment flooded her. She hoped he didn't think she'd done it on purpose.

When she looked up again, Daniel was sipping his drink, expressionless. More embarrassment flooded Mia—she must be imagining this *heat*. The man had been married, and he'd probably taken countless lovers since. She knew how voracious he was in bed. A man like that would crave stimulation.

Now he frowned. 'Mia…'

Right. The baby. *Lexi.*

She cursed herself. She couldn't blame the baby for baby brain when she was eighteen months old.

Suddenly an expression crossed Daniel's face. Something like shock. He put his glass down on the table and moved his leg, sitting forward. 'Did you lie about the miscarriage?'

It took a second for his question to register, and then

Mia recoiled in horror. 'No, of course not. How could you think such a thing?'

Daniel stood up. He waved a hand in the direction of the bedroom. 'Well, how else can you explain the baby?'

The baby.

All of Mia's protective instincts snapped into place. 'Her name is Lexi. She's your daughter.'

Daniel's jaw clenched. 'A daughter I had no idea existed until about an hour ago.'

Mia deflated. He was right. She forced herself to meet that penetrating grey gaze. 'I did have a miscarriage. I would never have lied about that.'

'Go on.'

In a rush, Mia explained. 'It was twins. But I didn't know that at the time. And they didn't pick it up in the hospital. I only discovered I was still pregnant about a month later, when I knew something wasn't right.'

'So why didn't you tell me then?'

Because she'd found out on the day of Daniel's dynastic wedding. The official engagement announcement had come about a week after Mia had miscarried. He'd wasted no time in moving on with his life. And even though the wedding had been a fairly modest affair, and conducted in the office of a *mairie*, it had still made headlines all over the world.

She avoided his eye, feeling as if he could see all the way through her to where her hurt still resided. 'I wasn't very well. I had an infection. I almost lost Lexi. To be perfectly honest, the reason I didn't tell you when I realised I was still pregnant was because I didn't know if everything would be okay.'

'Clearly it was.'

Mia nodded, forcing herself to look at him again. 'Yes, thankfully. As the pregnancy progressed I got healthier, and the birth was without complication.'

'And your reason for not telling me then was…?'

Mia looked at him, wondering how on earth she could start to try and explain a process that she didn't even fully understand herself, even though she'd been through it. How to explain how her world had contracted to only her baby and how every day had been a feat of survival and coping and learning how to navigate a new world. A terrifying one. Not to mention the bone-crippling exhaustion. The constant mental fog. She felt it would sound paltry. Weak.

She said, 'I did think of contacting you a few times, but Paris seemed very far away and I was afraid of what the news would do to your marriage…your wife. The longer it went on the harder it got to make contact, and then when I did try I didn't get very far.'

He frowned. 'You haven't been in Paris all this time?'

She shook her head. 'No, I moved down to the south of France after we…after I lost the baby. A fresh start. A friend has a small modelling agency down there. I did some catalogue work. That's where I discovered I was still pregnant and had Lexi. I've only been back in Paris a few weeks.'

Daniel seemed to take a moment to absorb this. As the silence grew, so did Mia's sense of guilt. The full enormity of what she'd kept from the father of her child was hitting her now.

Defensively she said, 'Based on your reaction to

finding out about the pregnancy the first time around, I knew you weren't likely to be more receptive the second time.'

Daniel wanted to say that that wasn't fair, but he knew he had little defence against her statement. Mia had turned up in his office about a month after they'd split up, pale and visibly nervous.

Much to his disgust—because usually women… lovers…didn't linger in his mind or memory when he was done with them—seeing Mia again had pre-cipitated a surge of desire as strong as if they'd never parted. Much the same as when he'd seen her again this evening.

He'd just arranged to have a meeting with Sophie Valois to discuss the proposed marriage, and seeing Mia again in the flesh had made him realise that his decision to go ahead with the meeting with Sophie had had a lot to do with her. Because she'd got too close. She'd got under his skin in a way that no other lover had, prompting him to remember that he didn't *want* any emotional entanglements. And that perhaps an ar-ranged marriage was the perfect solution to carving out a life free of such risks.

His parents had been unloving, cruel and dysfunc-tional, breeding in him a desire never to repeat their mistakes or visit their toxicity on another generation. The grief of losing his sister had almost destroyed him, and guilt for his part in her death had given him a life-long sense, rightly or wrongly, that he didn't deserve the happiness that most people seemed to expect and take for granted as their due.

And yet the day that Mia had seen the article about his proposed engagement in the paper, when he'd seen the hurt in her eyes, he'd suddenly resented the guilt and the grief and the darkness that had dogged him all his life. The duty he'd taken on. The responsibilities. A tantalising vision of another kind of life had existed in his mind's eye for a moment, before he'd reminded himself that he was not that person. He was not the kind of man who could offer an uncomplicated life to Mia. Nor did he want to—no matter how much he'd enjoyed his time with her.

When Mia had robustly denied she'd been looking for anything *'more'*, he'd told himself he'd imagined the hurt in her eyes. She was the most independent woman he'd ever met. He'd walked away, vowing never to let another woman get that close again. It had made him yearn briefly for an existence that wasn't possible for him. It wasn't his due.

Daniel had spent the next month restoring his sense of control. Realising that while he'd been consumed with Mia he'd taken his eye off the business and that his attention was needed to get it back on track. He'd buried himself in spreadsheets and projections. Meeting new jewellery designers. But nothing had seemed to pierce the numbness.

Until she'd appeared in his office that fateful day. Hair pulled back. Wearing jeans and a soft long-sleeved top. Looking pale.

He'd had to battle a primal urge to haul her against him, to trace every contour of her body with his hands and mouth until she was breathless and pliant in his arms.

His helpless reaction had made him curt. 'What do you want, Mia?'

Because, ultimately, everyone wanted *something* from him, and in that moment he'd desperately wanted Mia to show him that she was just as avaricious as every other woman he'd ever met—that she couldn't be all that different.

And then she'd blurted out, 'I'm pregnant.'

Daniel's insides had turned to ice. *Pregnant. A baby.* The very scenario he'd vowed to avoid. In that moment all he'd been able to think about was the cavernous dark chateau where he'd grown up. His mother's twisted angry face. His father's endless cold dismissal. And, worst of all, his sister, floating facedown…

He'd said to Mia, 'How can you be pregnant? We used protection every time we were together.'

Mia had blushed and said, 'We did…but the last few times…maybe we weren't as careful as usual…'

And his conscience had stung, because she'd been right. As zealous as he usually was about protection, the heat between him and Mia had been growing, not diminishing, and there had been moments when passion had overcome the need to be cautious.

Daniel looked at Mia now, disentangling the past from the present. He knew he owed her an explanation for why he'd behaved so coldly that day—the day she'd come to tell him of the pregnancy, only to then, a short time later, double over with pain in his office, which had precipitated a dash to the hospital and the subsequent miscarriage.

He'd found out about the pregnancy and lost it within hours.

He'd tried to explain at the hospital that day, but it had been too late. She hadn't wanted to hear and he hadn't blamed her.

'The reason I wasn't…receptive to the idea of a baby was because I'd never had any intention of having children. A family…' His voice felt rusty from the weight of past memories.

Mia unfolded her arms. She frowned. 'But what about the business? If you don't have children, what happens to Devilliers?'

'Things have changed. The brand name will exist whether it's in the family or not.'

'You would let the business go?'

'No, I would ensure that the brand lives on no matter what, whether that's through a bloodline or via a trust.'

'I wondered…you didn't have a child with your wife.'

Daniel folded his arms. '*Ex*-wife. And, no. We didn't. The marriage wasn't about that.'

He could see that that had sparked Mia's curiosity but he had no intention of going into detail about his marriage.

It was slowly sinking in, amidst the onslaught of too many memories and the resurgence of a very inconvenient desire, that he was a father. It was a fait accompli. A situation he'd never envisaged allowing to happen. Yet it had.

'Look,' Mia said, 'I just wanted to let you know… I'm sorry I didn't tell you before now. I should have made more of an effort. You'll probably want to do a DNA test—'

'Why?'

'To prove that she's yours…'

'I know she's a Devilliers.'

Now Mia folded her arms. 'Well, she's not a Devilliers. She's a Forde.'

Daniel felt something very alien take root inside him. A sense of possessiveness. Proprietorial.

'She's a Devilliers, Mia. Heiress to a vast fortune. Whether you like it or not.'

Mia felt a cold finger trace down her spine. She hadn't expected Daniel to accept so quickly that Lexi was his. She'd been prepared for horror, shock, and then denial. She'd assumed that he would want to distance himself as quickly as possible.

She realised now she'd totally underestimated him and his reaction. And that she'd hoped that once she'd told him she would feel she had done her duty and could get on with her life.

She should have known better. She'd been ridiculously naive. Which was galling, because she'd lost any sense of naivety a long time ago.

'I don't expect anything from you, Daniel. I can support Lexi on my own. I just wanted you to know. And of course I would have told you eventually. I grew up not knowing my father. I wouldn't have wanted that for Lexi.'

'Yet she's been without a father for eighteen months already.'

Mia's face grew hot, and she felt panicky. She didn't

like the look on Daniel's face. 'You just said you've never wanted a family. Children. That day in the hospital you told me that the miscarriage was probably for the best.'

Daniel's jaw clenched and unclenched. 'Because after the childhood I experienced I never wanted to risk inflicting the same on another innocent child.'

Mia's panic drained away. 'You never spoke of your childhood or your family. It was that bad?'

Daniel was grim. 'It was worse.'

Mia had always had an impression of him standing apart from everyone else. She'd used to tease him that it was because he thought he was better than everyone else around him, and for the most part he was certainly superior—intellectually, physically. But now she saw something else. That perhaps his past had kept him apart from others.

There was something there she wanted to tease out, but not while she was under that grey gaze. The evening was catching up with her.

She said, 'It's late. Lexi might wake again. I need to watch her and make sure she's okay. You should go back to your party.'

Daniel didn't move. Mia was afraid he was going to refuse to leave. But then he glanced at his watch. And then back at her. 'This discussion isn't over, Mia. I'll contact you tomorrow.'

'But—'

He stopped in the act of pulling on his jacket. 'But what?'

Mia knew it was futile to argue. 'Okay.'

Once Daniel had left, Mia couldn't relax. The

awareness in her body lingered like an overload of electricity that had nowhere to go. She went over and stood at the window, just in time to see Daniel's tall, broad figure emerging from her building and then disappearing again into the back of his sleek car.

She'd always wondered what he'd seen in her. She was nothing like the women from his world. She was somewhat of a free spirit. Independent. She wasn't polished. Intellectual. Socially savvy.

But from the moment they'd met a powerful force had surged between them. She'd been one of about ten models who'd been hired to go to a shoot for Devilliers. She'd been surprised to be cast, as she knew their advertising campaigns and they were very slick. Effortlessly glamorous. Sophisticated.

Mia had known she didn't really fit the brief, with her Californian aesthetic and her hair that refused to be tamed no matter how much product was used. In fact, she would have considered herself the very antithesis of a Devilliers model.

Yet there she was. Amongst lots of taller and far more angular models from Russia, the UK, France and Ukraine. She'd felt like the odd one out, with her more athletic shape and breasts that were probably three cup sizes bigger than everyone else's put together. She wasn't considered a plus-size model, but sample sizes were not her friend.

The stylist had kept passing her over for the shots and so, growing a little bored, Mia had found her way to the table where all the Devilliers jewels were laid out, guarded by at least two security guys.

Even though she had no love for jewellery, after a

toxic experience a couple of years previously, there was one necklace that had stood out—an oversize ruby in a simple setting. A markedly different style the other ornate designs. More modern.

Mia had picked it up and fastened it around her neck and then looked in a mirror, lifting her hair and twisting it so that she could see how it looked. She'd grinned at herself, because of course it looked a bit ridiculous against her plain white T-shirt, and then she'd almost had a heart attack when a deep voice near her had said, 'It suits you.'

Mia had dropped her hands and whirled around to see the tallest, most breathtakingly handsome man she'd ever laid eyes on. He'd been wearing a three-piece suit in steel-grey, and that was when she'd noticed his eyes. They'd reminded her of the slate-grey clouds that rolled in from the Pacific Ocean during storms.

Her heart had stopped for a long moment before palpitating back to life at double its regular rate. Mia had thought that after her experiences she was immune to a ridiculously handsome face, but evidently there was no accounting for taste. She'd assumed that he was one of the executives overseeing the shoot. She'd smiled sheepishly and reached behind her for the catch to take off the necklace, but he'd stepped forward.

'Let me.'

She'd turned around again and he'd stepped up behind her, his scent reaching her nostrils, subtly potent and unashamedly masculine. She'd felt a flutter deep in her belly.

He'd said, 'Lift your hair.'

She'd pulled it up and his fingers had brushed the back of her neck, turning the flutter into a tsunami of sensation.

He'd expertly undone the necklace and taken it off. Their eyes had met in the mirror, where she'd noticed he towered several inches over her. A tall woman herself, it wasn't every day she met a man taller than her. But he had to be at least six foot four.

She'd only noticed then that the security guards had melted away discreetly. But before she'd been able to wonder about that, and who this man was, he'd said, 'Come over to the set. I want to try something.'

Mia had turned to face him. She'd gestured to her clothes—jeans and the white T-shirt. 'The stylist hasn't dressed me yet.' And she'd suspected had no intention of it. But she kept that to herself.

'You're perfect as you are.'

His accent was unmistakably French, but he spoke English fluently. He'd led her over to where there was a black backdrop and suddenly, as if a silent message had been issued, Mia had been surrounded by a flurry of activity. She'd been perched on a stool and over the next hour photographed with her hair up, down, and in various combinations of jewels. Necklaces—the one she'd tried on first, and then others—earrings, bracelets and rings.

And all the time the enigmatic man in the suit had watched her. It had been deeply unsettling, but also exciting. As if there was a line of tension tugging between only them, drawing her eyes back to him over and over again, to find he was looking at her with that impenetrable slate-grey gaze.

When the shoot had wrapped Mia had still been none the wiser as to who the man was, or why he'd instructed her to be photographed in the most inappropriate clothing to showcase the famous Devilliers jewels.

She'd gathered up her things and tried not to feel self-conscious about the fact that she was the only model who hadn't been dressed in designer dresses, feeling fairly certain she wouldn't be seeing any of the pictures they'd taken of her on a billboard any time soon.

And then, just when she'd hated herself for wondering where the man had disappeared to, she'd turned around to leave and had run straight into a steel wall. A very broad steel wall.

His hands had gone to her arms, to steady her and she'd looked up. He had been smiling and she'd almost lost her life. His mouth was perfect. Surprisingly sensual for a man, yet not remotely *pretty*. Sexy.

He'd taken his hands down and said, 'I never introduced myself. I'm Daniel Devilliers, and I would very much like you to join me for dinner this evening.'

CHAPTER THREE

MIA HADN'T JOINED Daniel for dinner that first evening. She'd been in too much shock to find out that he was *Mr Devilliers*. Not just some suited executive. That he was the scion of one of the oldest and most established jewellery brands in the world. A billionaire. An entitled and privileged man. Practically aristocracy.

That alone had raised about a million red flags for Mia. She wasn't in his league. Never would be. Never wanted to be. She'd been burnt badly before, by someone who had come from a rarefied privileged world, when for a moment she'd believed that she could be part of it too. She'd never forgiven herself for that weakness.

Daniel couldn't know that part of her reluctance was not only because he came with the baggage he did—wealth, entitlement, et cetera—but also because she'd slept with precisely one man in her life. And that man had decimated her by winning her trust and then betraying her when she was at her most vulnerable.

But she hadn't counted on Daniel's single-minded determination to seduce her, and in spite of all those red flags he'd finally, fatally, worn her down.

He'd sent her flowers with a note.

Mia
I want you, on your terms.
I don't play games.
Call me.
Daniel

There had been something unexpectedly humbling about the fact that he was willing to let her dictate how the affair would play out, and when she'd told him that she didn't want any part of his world he hadn't balked.

Yet she'd dreaded the moment Daniel would realise how inexperienced she was—and, worse, that she really didn't find sex all that exciting. She'd even told him, hoping it would put him off. But he'd only grown more determined. As if she'd laid down a challenge to prove to her that her inexperience didn't matter and that she was a sexual, sensual woman.

Even now Mia's blood grew hot just at the thought of that first night they'd slept together. The experience had altered her in a very fundamental way. He'd returned something to her that she hadn't even been aware she'd missed. The knowledge that there was nothing wrong with her. That her previous bad experience had had nothing to do with her and everything to do with her first, very ungenerous lover.

Daniel had shown her how intoxicating it was to be with a man who didn't let his ego get in the way. How it felt to be put first, before a man's own pleasure...

They'd conducted their affair without attracting any attention. Under the radar. Low-key. And Mia had got the impression that Daniel found it somewhat...refreshing. Hanging out in her apartment... Eating in modest **restaurants**... She'd always refused any invitation to go beyond their little bubble, knowing that at all costs her self-preservation depended on not getting seduced into Daniel's world.

But in the end keeping strict boundaries had done nothing to stop her from falling—

'We're here, Miss Forde.'

Mia blinked. The sleek car had come to a stop outside the Devilliers *salon* on Place Vendôme. It was quiet this evening. No glittering guests or flashes of light from the paparazzi. The party was well and truly over.

Mia sucked in a breath as the driver got out and came around to her door. Daniel had sent her a curt text earlier.

My driver will pick you up at seven and bring you to my apartment.

She'd been tempted to text back that she couldn't come, but of course that would have been immature, and she did need to discuss Lexi with Daniel. After all, she'd set this chain of events into motion. And she should have probably done it a lot sooner.

All day, Daniel's revelations about his family had buzzed in her head, making her want to know more.

The driver opened her door, cutting off her thoughts. She got out. The autumn air was chilly enough to herald the winter season just around the corner.

She'd dressed carefully, wanting to feel somewhat put-together in Daniel's presence. She wore a rust-coloured soft jersey dress with a wide leather belt.

High-heeled boots. Her leather jacket on top. She'd pulled her hair back into a rough bun, eschewed any jewellery.

Daniel had always found it highly amusing that Mia had zero interest in jewellery. And she'd never told him why. Never told him that her ex-boyfriend had given her a gift of a diamond necklace which she'd interpreted naively as evidence that he really loved her.

Until she'd discovered it was just cubic zirconia and that it had meant nothing at all. It had been an empty, cynical gesture and she'd fallen for it.

To the left of the *salon* there was a set of discreet doors. They opened now and a uniformed butler stepped out. 'Ms Forde?'

Mia went over to him.

He said in perfect English, 'Please allow me to show you up to the apartment.'

She followed him into a black-and-white-tiled reception hall. A massive crystal chandelier dominated the almost cathedral-like space, and the biggest vase she'd ever seen sat on a polished round table, filled with exotic blooms that sent out a subtle and very expensive-smelling scent.

A grand marble staircase led upstairs, but the butler walked over to an elevator. The doors were open. Mia got in.

The lift ascended and Mia's insides dropped like a stone. The thought of coming face to face with Daniel again was daunting, and she cursed herself. She should be more prepared. A man like Daniel Devilliers didn't take prisoners.

The lift stopped and the doors opened onto another

reception space. Light colours and a parquet floor gave it a classically elegant feel. The butler took her coat and Mia became aware that the soft jersey material of her dress suddenly felt very clingy. Especially around her breasts, belly, hips and bum.

But it was too late. A door was opening and Daniel appeared on the threshold, dressed in a three-piece suit.

He addressed the butler. 'Thank you, Paul.' And then Mia, eyes narrowed. 'You didn't bring Lexi.'

Mia shook her head. 'No. It's not a good idea to disrupt her routine. She goes down for the night around now.'

'Who is taking care of her?'

After eighteen months of being solely responsible for her child, Mia chafed at the proprietorial tone in Daniel's voice. 'My friend Simone is babysitting again.'

'The one who rang you in a panic when there was no need to panic?'

Mia smiled sweetly. 'Yes, that's the one.'

Daniel stood back. 'Please, come in.'

She felt ridiculously nervous. Very aware of Daniel's physicality and scent in an almost animalistic way. She held herself tensely as she walked past him into the apartment.

Daniel watched as Mia looked around the formal reception room, taking in the big abstract paintings on the walls—the only modernity in the otherwise classically designed space, which was dotted with antiques. It suddenly felt a little overdone with her here. As if she was highlighting its fussiness with her far more relaxed aesthetic.

He could smell her unique scent. Light and fresh. Citrussy but with a hint of musk and roses. And her body...tall and strong...curvier than was fashionable. It was probably the reason she'd never made it into the upper echelons of modelling—because she didn't have the androgynous aesthetic that was required by most fashion houses.

The material of her dress clung to every dip and curve, reminding Daniel all too easily of how those curves had felt under his hands. *Under his mouth.* He cursed himself silently and diverted his mind from dangerous territory.

Mia had always been happy to achieve a certain level of success without hungering for more. Something that had fascinated Daniel who, ever since he was born, had felt a constant pressure to attain ever higher levels of success and wealth.

The couple of months he'd spent with Mia was the first time he could remember in his life when he'd taken his foot off the accelerator. It had been a revelation. And, perversely, once he hadn't been working with such tunnel vision, he'd been able to see areas where the business could do with improvement.

'Would you like a drink?'

He remembered his manners at the last moment. This woman had always had the ability to distract him.

'A small glass of white wine would be nice, thank you.'

Daniel poured her drink and went over to hand it to her. A rogue devil inside him made sure their fingers touched. *Zing.* Wide, startled green eyes met his. Lust bit into Daniel's gut. She still felt it too.

Mia snatched the glass and stepped back. Cheeks deep pink. Avoiding his eye.

Daniel went back to the drinks table and poured himself something stronger than wine. He gestured to a couch. 'Please, make yourself comfortable.'

Mia looked at the furniture warily, as if it might be some kind of trap. But then she sat down, her movements effortlessly graceful. He remembered that she'd wanted to be a dancer, but a teenage knee injury had put a stop to those dreams.

He took a seat on the other side of a low coffee table. Before he could speak, she said, 'I'm sorry for disrupting your party last night.'

'Are you?'

An expression of guilt crossed her face. She'd never been good at hiding her feelings. That reminder caught at Daniel's gut.

She said, 'I know it was a big night for you and Devilliers, but it genuinely seemed my best opportunity to get to you.'

'What if I hadn't got divorced? How long would you have made me wait to learn that I have a daughter?'

Something jagged entered Mia's belly. If he hadn't got divorced he would have been there with his wife last night. Petite and dark. As refined as him. Not that she'd looked them up. *Much.* Shame filled her at her weakness, her need to torture herself by looking them up on the internet.

She had to admit the truth. 'I probably wouldn't

have come last night but, as I said, I would have tried to contact you somehow. I knew you had to know about Lexi, married or not.'

'I should have known about her as soon as you knew you were still pregnant.'

Mia clutched the glass in her hands. 'I found out the day of your wedding.' She shut her mouth, aghast that she'd let that slip out. She stood up, feeling agitated now. 'I told you—I wasn't even sure I wouldn't lose Lexi. What would have been the point of telling you and disrupting your marriage only for something to go wrong again? I felt I had good reason to say nothing. And then, when she was born…it was seriously over-whelming. Holding down a job, becoming a mother… just getting through each day was a challenge.'

Daniel frowned. 'You can't blame me for not being there to help when you deliberately excluded me.'

Anger mixed with guilt surged inside Mia. 'And you can't blame *me* for feeling reluctant to tell you after what you said about losing the baby.'

Daniel's face turned stony. 'I told you… I had good reason not to want to create a family.'

Mia moved behind the seat, as if that might pro-vide some protection from this conversation. When he didn't elaborate, she said, 'I think I deserve to know what you're talking about. We have a child together.'

Daniel ran a hand through his hair, jaw clenching. He stood up too, and moved over to the window. The suit emphasised his broad back and slim waist. The long legs.

His reluctance to speak was palpable, but as if he knew she was right, he said eventually, 'I grew up with privilege—extreme privilege. I would never deny that. But my parents were of the view that once we had that inherited privilege nothing else was required. Like love. Or caring. Or nurturing. We were just left…left to our own devices.'

'You and your sister?'

Daniel turned around to face her. He nodded. His face was in shadow. She couldn't read his expression. It was disconcerting.

Mia asked, 'How old was your sister when she died?'

Daniel's voice was clipped. 'Six. I was nine.'

Mia's heart twisted. 'She was so young—how did she—?'

But Daniel cut her off. 'It was a long time ago. The point is that we might not have been beaten, or abused in any tangible way, but what we—*I* witnessed was something unbelievably cruel and cold. Neglect is its own form of torture. I don't have the tools to create a happy family, but I will not shirk my responsibility to Lexi.'

That assertion sent a prickle of foreboding down Mia's spine, but the tone in Daniel's voice was so bleak it caught in her chest.

She bit her lip before asking a little hesitantly, 'Is that why your marriage broke up? Because your wife wanted children?'

He stepped out of the shadows and into the light. She was surprised to see a flicker of something at the edge of his mouth. 'No, that's not why we broke up. My ex-wife may well decide to have children in the future, but it wasn't ever going to be part of our arrangement.'

Mia shook her head. 'So why bother getting married in the first place, if it was going to end so soon?'

'It was a business arrangement. We agreed to the length of our marriage from the very start.'

'Oh.' That didn't mean that he hadn't wanted his wife, that they hadn't still enjoyed—

'I can hear your thoughts from here, Mia.' Daniel's tone was dry.

She hated it that he still had that ability—it made her want to scowl.

He said, 'Not that it's any of your business, but my wife and I didn't consummate the marriage.'

Mia hated the burst of relief in her solar plexus. 'What do you mean?'

He arched a brow. 'Do you really need an explanation?'

She blushed. 'No, but…why?'

Daniel said, 'Because she's gay, and her family are ultra-conservative. She never would have received her inheritance if they'd found out. The marriage was purely to fulfil the agreement and throw up a smoke-screen to distract her family. That's why she leaked it to the papers. She was afraid that I would renege on the agreement. When we met, she explained her situation, and I agreed to marry her and then divorce her once she was sure she'd receive her inheritance.'

So he'd married her as a favour? Mia absorbed that. It was huge.

And they hadn't slept together.

Mia hadn't slept with anyone since Daniel—unsurprisingly. But she didn't doubt that, in spite of his chaste marriage, he'd notched up several conquests, so her relief was a little misplaced. She'd be incredibly naive if she believed he'd been celibate all this time.

Not that any of his affairs had appeared in the media. He was too sophisticated for that, and the Devilliers brand certainly wouldn't have stood for it.

'So you are still modelling, then?'

Mia welcomed the distraction from imagining Daniel in bed with other women. 'Yes, I'm back with my agent here in Paris. I did some pregnancy modelling in the South of France, until I became too big. After Lexi was born I worked part-time in a café, until I was in some kind of shape to try modelling again.'

Daniel's eyes dipped to her body, and Mia cursed her choice of words. She felt self-conscious under that far too assessing gaze. After all, this was a man who was an expert at spotting imperfections in his jewels. Mia knew she was far from perfect, and that whatever had attracted him to her in the first place had burnt out long ago. She was very different now.

His gaze lifted again. 'I should have been supporting you.'

She felt another dart of guilt. 'We were okay. I had savings. We didn't need much to live on. We had a nice apartment near the seafront.'

And yet the whole time she hadn't been able to relax fully, conscious of Daniel in Paris, unaware that he was a father.

Mia took a sip of wine, hoping it might make her feel she was on more of an even keel. Daniel had always made her feel too aware of herself.

She said, 'Look, I truly don't expect anything from

you, Daniel. I just wanted you to know…about Lexi. We can support ourselves.'

Mia chose not to think about what Daniel had said last night about Lexi being a Devilliers. She hoped he wouldn't mention it again.

'So…what? That's it? I'll just get to see my daughter growing up from a distance while you work to make ends meet?' He shook his head, before answering himself. 'That is not how this will go, Mia.'

Panic fluttered in Mia's breast. 'We really don't need anything.'

Daniel emitted a harsh-sounding laugh. 'If I didn't already know you, I would think this is all an act. A ruse to extract as much as you can by feigning otherwise. But because I know you, and know how independent you are—to a fault—I know this isn't a ruse.'

Daniel took a step closer to where Mia stood, an intense expression she'd never seen before on his face.

'She's my daughter.'

A daughter you never wanted.

It trembled on Mia's tongue, but she stopped the words from falling out. That wasn't fair either.

Feeling nervous, she said, 'So what are you saying…? You want to be involved with Lexi? We can draw up some kind of custody arrangement, Daniel. I wouldn't stop you trying to see your daughter or being involved in her life. That's why I'm here.'

Daniel shook his head. 'Not good enough, Mia. You've kept her from me since her birth. I know I said I never wanted a family, but that was before Lexi existed. She's my daughter and she's a Devilliers.'

Icicles pierced Mia's heart. 'So what are you saying?'

'I'm telling you now that I won't expect anything less than full access to my daughter, and the most expedient and practical way for that to happen is for us to marry.'

Daniel was surprised at how easily those words had tripped off his tongue. He hadn't even consciously decided *what* the best solution was, but something about Mia's proximity and the tangled emotions she was evoking, not to mention the memories, had prompted him to say what he had.

And now he found that he couldn't even drum up much regret or even shock at his words. But he could see shock on Mia's face. And fear. And—

Suddenly her face blanked. It was as if she was aware she was giving too much away and had learnt to hide behind a bland mask. It irritated Daniel intensely.

She was pale. She shook her head. 'No way.'

Daniel was not used to being refused much—in fact this woman was the only one who had ever made him work for anything. He had a flashback to his feeling of triumph when she'd finally capitulated and agreed to go on a date with him. Not to mention the first time he'd slept with her. And every subsequent time. He'd never experienced chemistry like it. Before or since. He'd been desperate. Unable to get her out of his head. Consumed by wanting her. Insatiable.

With an effort, he pushed the rogue memories down deep. That was the past. They were dealing with the present and the future, and Daniel was sure that the madness that had existed between them before would be well burnt out by now. It couldn't still exist.

Yet your blood hums even now. And you can't take your eyes off her.

He scowled.

Mia was taking a step back, shaking her head. 'I am not marrying you, Daniel. It's a ridiculous suggestion. I shouldn't be surprised, though—the last thing the Devilliers brand will want is a child and an ex-lover hanging about on the margins. Much neater to marry and incorporate us into your world.'

'And what about Lexi? Doesn't she deserve to be part of her inheritance?'

Mia was agitated now, with colour in her cheeks. 'I wouldn't dream of denying her her inheritance. She can even have your name if she decides that she'd like that when she's old enough. We don't love each other, Daniel, and I know how you feel about having a family. So I won't go along with a charade just to help keep your world neat and tidy. Lexi deserves more and I deserve more.'

Daniel snorted. 'Since when did you turn into a romantic who wanted a perfect picket fence existence?'

Mia's cheeks went pinker. 'Maybe since I had a baby and my priorities changed. I'm under no illusions about what to expect from relationships, Daniel— believe me. But I want more for my daughter than to be a single parent with an absent father. At least she will know who you are and have some kind of relationship with you.'

She put down her glass and turned as if she was going to leave. With two steps Daniel put his hand on her arm, stopping her. He took his hand away, seriously afraid that he might haul her against his body and stop her speaking such nonsense by putting his mouth on hers.

'So you're telling me you'd marry someone else, but not the father of your child?'

'In order to have a happy life and home environment for Lexi? Maybe.'

Mia's head was spinning. *Marriage.* She wasn't sure what she'd expected, but it hadn't been that. To her eternal shame, her initial reaction when Daniel had said the word 'marry' had been a flutter of something very illicit deep inside. That part of herself that she'd packed in ice after his cruel words in the hospital that day. When he'd told her that losing their baby had been 'for the best'.

It wasn't much of a salve to know the reason why he'd believed that now. It only made her heart ache to learn about his less than idyllic childhood and losing his sister. Which was an indication that after only twenty-four hours in Daniel's company she was seriously in danger of losing her footing all over again.

She needed space from Daniel. He was seeing too much. Saying too many ridiculous things.

She blurted out the first thing she could think of to put space between them. 'I need to use the bathroom.'

Daniel pointed to a door at the other end of the vast room. 'There's a guest bathroom through that door.'

Mia walked towards the door, asking herself why she wasn't just leaving.

Because you created this situation and you need to deal with it. For Lexi's sake.

She found a plushly carpeted corridor on the other side of the door, and another door leading into an opulent bathroom. She shut herself inside, sucking in deep breaths to counteract the shock of Daniel's suggestion of marriage. Although 'suggestion' was far too gentle a word. It had been an assertion. An expectation that she would just agree.

She forced the panic down and told herself that Daniel couldn't force her to marry him. She'd never entertained any romantic notions of marriage after being brought up by a single parent, but her first boyfriend had exposed a weakness she'd denied to herself. A secret dream for a lifelong connection. Love. A family with two parents who loved and respected each other. She'd discovered she wanted more for her own children than a one-parent family, and that dream being unearthed had felt like a betrayal of her mother.

And then that dream had shattered at her feet anyway, when her ex-boyfriend had sneered at her, *'Of course this was never going to go anywhere, Mia, you're trailer trash.'*

Any notion of marriage she had now was far more pragmatic, and she'd vowed that if it ever happened it would be with someone who she respected and trusted and who wouldn't hurt her. Not intentionally, at least.

Daniel Devilliers was literally the last man she would marry. While of course Mia wanted Lexi to know her father, and have a relationship with him, she wasn't going to allow it to happen in a sham marriage.

Mia had made a huge error of judgement once in her life, and had come close to another lapse with Daniel the last time. It wouldn't happen again.

CHAPTER FOUR

'HAVE YOU EATEN?'

Of all the things Mia might have expected Daniel to say to her on her return from the bathroom, feeling marginally more composed, it hadn't been that.

He said, 'I've been in back-to-back meetings all day and the chef has made me something—would you join me?'

Much to her chagrin, Mia felt her stomach respond to that question with a slight hollow ache. She remembered her appetite had never failed to amaze Daniel but, as much as she longed to say no, she hadn't eaten much herself that day.

She put her light-headedness down to that, and not the man standing a few feet away who had just upended her world with one word.

Marriage.

As much as she wanted to leave right now, she knew they had to talk about this and get it sorted.

'Okay,' she said reluctantly, 'if it's not putting your staff to too much trouble.'

Daniel held out a hand, indicating that Mia should

precede him out of the room. 'Not at all,' he replied smoothly.

When they walked into an elegant dining room, Mia noted that he'd taken off his jacket and tie. But he was still wearing a waistcoat which drew attention to his slim waist and lean torso. He managed to look both debauched and yet elegant.

Maybe it was down to the fact that she'd slept with him, so she knew just how debauched he could be...

Not where she wanted her mind to go now. Not when she was feeling so exposed.

There was a long table and two places set at one end. Daniel held out a chair for her and she sat down, trying not to inhale his scent, which was far too evocative.

A middle-aged woman appeared with starters. Mia's mouth watered when she saw a pear and watercress salad with walnuts.

When the woman had left, Mia said, 'I wasn't expecting anything fancy.'

'It's not. Eat up.'

Mia took a bite of salad, the sweetness of the pear contrasting nicely with the peppery watercress and walnut. She had to bite back a groan of appreciation. She'd got used to throwing together any old thing to eat, after feeding Lexi, and it had been a long time since she'd had anything remotely sophisticated.

Daniel poured more wine into Mia's glass and poured some for himself. 'You never did tell me where your interest in food came from,' he said.

Mia was suspicious of this innocuous direction in conversation, but she went with it. She'd made lots of meals for Daniel in her little apartment. She'd never seen food as sensual, or a precursor to passion, until she'd met him.

'My mother. She was a great cook. An amateur, though. She taught me to appreciate it. I think she would have loved to train to be a chef, but we didn't have the money.'

'It must have been tough for her…being a single parent.'

Mia nodded. 'She had to work hard to make ends meet.'

Daniel sat back. 'And yet in spite of that you're willing to let our daughter go through the same experience?'

Mia glared at Daniel. She'd walked into that one. She should have known he wasn't making idle conversation because he was genuinely interested. This was all part of his strategy.

'It won't be similar at all. Because Lexi will know you and I earn a lot more than my mother did, so I can support us comfortably.'

'Until you can't.'

'What's that supposed to mean?'

More staff appeared, to clear away the starter plates, and Mia forced a smile. When they were gone, she looked at Daniel.

'What happens when you don't want to model any more?' he asked. 'What will you do then?'

His question struck a nerve, because in all honesty Mia had been wondering the same thing herself. But he didn't know that she was feeling ambivalent about going back into modelling.

She lifted her chin. 'I can worry about that when the time comes. I might go back to school…get a degree.' She'd always been interested in the arts, but the death of her mother and the need to survive had put paid to going to college.

'And who would take care of Lexi?'

'As you'll be in her life, I'm sure we can come to some arrangement.'

Although, try as she might, Mia couldn't quite visualise Daniel standing at the school gates, waiting to pick up his daughter. It was more likely to be an assistant in a chauffered car.

Mia felt a pang at that. She wanted more for her daughter.

Their main courses arrived: tender fillet steaks with fresh vegetables and baby potatoes. Except Mia's legendary appetite was fading fast. After a few mouthfuls of the exquisitely cooked food, she put down her knife and fork.

Daniel looked at her. 'Not to your liking?'

Mia shook her head. 'No—I mean, *yes*. It's delicious. But…can we just talk about Lexi and come to some agreement? I don't want to be gone too long.'

Daniel put down his own knife and fork and picked up his wine. 'You really think it's that simple?'

No.

'I don't think we need to make it complicated.'

Daniel's jaw clenched. 'You made it complicated when you didn't tell me you were still pregnant.'

Mia fought down the guilt. 'I can't change the past. Can we please move on and discuss where we go from here?'

Daniel stood up and went over to the window. Darkness had fallen over the square outside. He turned around and said, 'I've already told you what will happen.'

Marriage.

Mia's insides knotted even tighter. She put her napkin on the table and stood up. 'If you're not going to make any attempt to be rational then I'm leaving.'

And not just because of what he was saying, but because the longer she spent in proximity to Daniel, the more she found herself remembering what it had been like to be with him. The more she found herself yearning for his touch again. Yearning to be consumed by passion. Which was the last thing she should be thinking about or wanting. That was what had led to here. This moment.

The realisation hit her that, no matter what, her life was entwined with Daniel's for ever. Entwined with a man who didn't want her any more but who felt a responsibility to a child he'd never wanted.

Mia returned to the drawing room and looked around for her bag. She couldn't see it.

'Where are you going?' asked Daniel.

She was feeling panicky. 'Where's my bag?'

Daniel walked over to the other side of the room and picked something up from a table near the door. 'Here it is.'

Mia walked over and moved to take her bag, but Daniel held it out of reach. 'You're really refusing to continue discussing this?'

She glared at him. 'There's nothing to discuss. We are not getting married.'

A muscle ticked in his jaw. 'So how do you see this panning out, then? Some loose arrangement where I get to be on the periphery of my daughter's life and see her intermittently?'

Mia dropped her hand. Daniel put her bag back down on the table. He folded his arms. *Why* did she have to be so aware of him? It was so inappropriate— and not conducive to clear-headed thinking.

Mia moved back into the room in order to try and put some distance between them. She even put a chair between them again. Not that Daniel looked as if he was about to bat it aside to get to her.

'Are you saying your feelings have changed and that you now want a family?' she asked.

'I now *have* a family.'

Mia blanched.

He had a family whether he liked it or not, and clearly he didn't like it, but he wasn't going to shirk his responsibility.

She shook her head. 'I will not marry just for the sake of it. But I'm perfectly happy to sit down and come to a mutual decision about visitation and access to your daughter.'

Daniel's face became stony. 'I won't agree to anything that's not legally binding. If we take this to court, Mia, it'll cost a lot of money.'

Mia stepped out from behind the chair. 'If it goes to court that'll be down to one person—*you*. And I don't think Devilliers will look too favourably on their CEO's personal life being splashed all over the press. It works both ways.'

Daniel felt frustration rise at the same time as admiration. Mia had always stood up to him. One of the few people who ever had. And she was right. If they went to court it would be messy, and the board were still letting it be known that they were less than happy with his short-lived marriage.

Daniel wanted to usher a modern era into the Devilliers brand but announcing a secret child, an ex-lover and a potential legal battle for custody, while certainly very modern, was not going in the right direction.

As if sensing that she'd got through to him, Mia said, 'I'm fully prepared to go through mediation so we can both be satisfied. I'll sign anything you want once it's reasonable. I want what's best for Lexi.'

Daniel's body tightened at the word *satisfied*. It reminded him that he'd never felt as satisfied as he had with this woman. Every time. She'd been like a sorceress. And it hadn't even been down to experience. She was probably the most inexperienced lover he'd ever slept with. Not a virgin, but not far off. And, inexplicably for such a beautiful sexy woman, seriously lacking in confidence.

The first time they'd slept together she'd been so nervous, and when he'd made her come... The look on her face had been one of wonder, gratitude, relief, and a very carnal awakening. It had blasted apart any notion he might have had that conducting an affair with

Mia Forde was going to be like every other relationship he'd had. Short and satisfying but ultimately fleeting.

He still woke sometimes in the middle of the night amongst sweat-soaked sheets, his body pulsing with desire for that moment all over again. It definitely hadn't been fleeting and forgettable...

Daniel focused on the other word she'd mentioned: *mediation*. The thought of sitting around a table with a bunch of men and women in suits made something curdle in his gut. He might not have ever set out to have a family, but seeing Lexi had awoken something long dormant inside him: the desire to protect. And seeing Mia again had revived something far more potent and adult: a desire to *have* her again.

Everything Mia was suggesting was eminently reasonable, but Daniel knew that *reasonable* was not good enough. Not by a long shot. Last time they'd been together Mia had resolutely refused to enter his world, but now things were very different and she really didn't have a choice. He wouldn't accept anything less.

Mia didn't like the look on Daniel's face. His gaze was narrowed on her and it was far too calculating. She should have known this wouldn't be easy.

'Daniel, look—'

He cut her off. 'It's getting late. You should probably return to Lexi. We can continue this discussion another time. After all, there's no rush, is there? Unless you're planning on leaving Paris again?'

Mia shook her head, immediately suspicious at Daniel's volte face. 'No, that's why I came back. To tell you about Lexi. To be here so that we could make an arrangement that works for all of us.'

Daniel picked up her bag again and held it out. 'I'm sure we can do that. I'll have my driver take you home.'

Mia walked forward and took her bag, a little winded at the speed with which Daniel was despatching her. Her little finger touched Daniel's hand and a crackle of electricity sparked up her arm. She looked at him, but he seemed oblivious.

He must have sent a telepathic message to his butler because the man appeared in the doorway with Mia's jacket.

Daniel took it and held it up. 'Here, let me.'

Mia turned around and let Daniel help her put the jacket on. Did his fingers linger at the back of her neck? Or maybe she was craving his touch so much that she was just imagining it. It sent a shiver of awareness down her spine anyway.

She turned around again quickly, mortified that she couldn't control her reactions around him. He walked her to the door and opened it.

She said, 'When will—?'

'I'll call you. We'll make a plan.'

He sounded positively benign, which Mia didn't trust for a second. This was the man who had managed to pick away at all of her very strong defences to seduce her, and then, even when she'd given in on her terms—or so she'd believed—had still managed to prove that any defence she'd thought she had left was an illusion, by making her fall for him.

It was only when she was almost at her apartment that she had a thought and went cold inside. Perhaps

Daniel had been so eager to get rid of her not because he had some nefarious plan, but because of something much more prosaic. He had a date.

It was all too easy for Mia to imagine some sleek blonde or sultry brunette being welcomed into his apartment. Daniel smiling, helping her to take off a coat, revealing a clinging silky dress. Smiling at her the way he'd used to smile at her. Full of wicked sensual promise.

Maybe he'd be considering the fact that even though he hadn't ever wanted a family, he now had the best of both words; the freedom to pursue his pleasures and an heir to pass on the Devilliers legacy to—which had to be a seductive prospect, no matter what he'd told Mia about the brand enduring with or without a bloodline.

It should be of some comfort to Mia that he seemed to be giving up his fight to convince her to marry him. Clearly he'd decided it was a mistake. But, much to her irritation, relief wasn't her predominant emotion. It was something far more ambiguous and harder to decipher.

About an hour later, Mia was changed and in soft comfy pyjamas. Lexi had woken, crying, and Mia had given her some milk, and now she was falling asleep again on Mia's shoulder.

The solid and surprisingly heavy form of her daughter was curled so trustingly into Mia that it almost broke her heart, thinking of her own mother and grieving her loss all over again.

She allowed herself to feel some measure of relief that Daniel knew now. Lexi deserved to know who her father was. To have some kind of relationship with him, hopefully. And Mia hadn't wanted history to repeat itself.

She'd never had the option of knowing her father. It had been the one subject that had been guaranteed to wind her normally mild-mannered mother up—any mention of who Mia's father was and she'd say, *'You don't need to know. It's better that you don't.'*

Mia sighed and moved from the window, taking Lexi into the bedroom and placing her back into her cot, before crawling into her own bed.

The fact that Daniel appeared to want to engage in getting to know Lexi was more than Mia had hoped for, based on how he'd reacted when she'd lost Lexi's twin. She'd never forget the stony look on his face. The way he'd been so cold.

Maybe when the dust settled and they came to an agreement about visitation et cetera, Mia could finally break out of this limbo she'd been in for two years and get on with her life. While Daniel Devilliers got on with his too. Surely over time she would be able to interact with him without feeling as if he could see right under her skin to where her blood hummed whenever he came close. To where her blood was humming even now, when he wasn't even close.

Mia cursed silently as she thumped her pillow and tried to get to sleep. But sleep was elusive, and when it did finally come it was full of dreams filled with carnal images that left her gritty-eyed and filled with a sense of aching frustration as dawn broke the next morning.

It had taken Mia a while to get going that morning. She was tired, and still unsettled after the last encounter with Daniel, and Lexi was fractious, so neither of them was on the best of form by the time Mia had buckled Lexi into her buggy and was heading out for a walk to the park and the playground.

But she was totally unprepared for the barrage of flashing lights and shouted questions as soon as she opened the door of her building. They were caught on the threshold, with half of Lexi's buggy on the other side of the door.

Mia was so shocked and stunned she couldn't move. Questions bombarded the air around her.

'Is Daniel Devilliers the father of your baby, Mia?'

'Where is Daniel? Did he know about the baby when he got married?'

'Are you back together?'

'Are you looking for a settlement?'

The only thing that broke Mia out of her stasis was the sight of one of the photographers pointing his lens directly at Lexi. Mia reacted with the fierce instinct of a mama bear. She pushed down the buggy's hood and rain cover and moved back inside the building.

As she did, she heard a sort of commotion at the back of the crowd. She saw a couple of photographers being bodily moved out of the way and then a figure appeared, tall and dark. And grim. Very grim.

Daniel.

He came to the doorway, his dark grey gaze moving over Mia and down to the pram. 'Are you okay?'

Mia nodded. 'I… I think so. We were just going out. Who…? What?'

How did they know?

Daniel said, 'I'll explain in a minute. Go back up to the apartment. I'll follow you.'

Before she could respond he turned around to face the mob, effectively shielding Mia and Lexi from sight, blocking the doorway. He spoke in rapid French to the paparazzi, and all Mia could make out was some reference to sending out a statement. Or an announcement.

She went to the lift and pressed the button. Daniel was still talking to the crowd in a clipped, authoritative voice.

When Mia was back in the apartment she put Lexi down with a bunch of toys to amuse herself. She went over to the window and sucked in a gasp. There was now what seemed to be hundreds of paparazzi outside. Cars trying to drive by were beeping. People were stopping, looking. One of the photographers had moved back and was now pointing his camera up at the building. He shouted something and pointed directly at Mia.

She pulled back, closing the shutters.

Lexi looked up. 'Mama?'

Mia bent down and lifted her up, a sick feeling pooling in her belly. 'Shh…it's okay, sweetheart.'

There was a sharp rap on the door and Mia went and opened it. Daniel came in, immediately and effortlessly dominating the space. He was wearing dark jeans and a dark top under a battered leather jacket. His jaw was stubbled. A sly voice whispered that perhaps he hadn't had time to shave after a night in bed with his date…

At that moment Lexi clapped her hands and said, 'Man!'

Mia pushed aside her rogue thoughts. 'What on

earth was that all about…? Why were they asking those questions? And how did you know to come?'

Daniel took his phone out of his pocket and did something to the screen before handing it to Mia. She put Lexi down and Lexi immediately toddled back over to her toys, seemingly oblivious to the tension.

Mia looked at the phone and the blood in her face and head drained south. She saw grainy pictures of her arriving in Place Vendôme yesterday evening, being admitted to Daniel's apartment.

And one blazing headline: *Qui est Mia Forde?*
Who is Mia Forde?

She looked at Daniel. 'How do they know my name? How do they know I even have a baby?'

Daniel was grim. 'I suspect one of the security guards who overheard our initial conversation at the party. Whoever it was must have sensed a story, leaked your name and the paparazzi dug up the rest. I'm making sure I get to the bottom of it. The press have been watching me more since the divorce, so that's why you were caught arriving last night. It's my fault.'

She looked at him, a suspicion forming. '*You* made sure they saw me arriving.'

She cursed her naivety. A man like Daniel never gave up until he got what he wanted. She should know. Lexi was proof of that.

He shook his head, his jaw clenching. 'Not intentionally, no. I wouldn't do that. I hate those vultures.'

Mia stopped. She had to grudgingly admit that it wasn't his style. He was ultra-discreet.

'I'm going to release a statement,' he said.

Mia's insides froze. 'Saying what?'

He looked at her. 'That we are happy to announce that we have a child together from a previous brief relationship and that we would appreciate privacy at this time.'

Mia was suspicious. 'That's all?'

Daniel nodded. 'There's no point trying to deny it. They'll only go digging and find out the truth anyway—and any other dirt they can find.'

Mia shivered to think of the invasive media picking apart her early life. It wouldn't be pretty. She'd grown up in a trailer park. Perfectly respectable, of course, but coupled with her association with Daniel Devilliers it would undoubtedly be portrayed in the worst light possible, to maximise damage to Devilliers.

Mia had never told Daniel anything about her past beyond very superficial stuff. Maybe now was the time to—

'My security team will get rid of the paparazzi, but now they know where you live, and that we have a child together, I can't see them leaving you alone for long, Mia.'

Mia promptly forgot about filling Daniel in about her past. 'We'll be under siege.'

'Yes, I'm afraid so.'

She sat down on the arm of her couch.

Lexi had been amusing herself, but walked over to Daniel now, and held out a unicorn. 'Man play?'

Mia held her breath, watching as Daniel went down on his haunches.

He took the unicorn from Lexi. 'What's her name?'

'Hossy!'

'Do you want to show me where she lives?'

Lexi nodded her head vigorously and grabbed Daniel's hand. She started pulling him over towards her play area.

Mia stood up. 'Lex—'

But Daniel quelled her with a look, telling her that he didn't mind, and for the second time in as many days Mia had to contend with the fact of having brought Daniel into their lives, and with the realisation that no matter how much or how little he engaged with them, there was now a new paradigm.

And she didn't like how watching him interact with Lexi was making her feel. Seriously vulnerable.

Okay, so he obviously wasn't used to kids—he was talking to Lexi as if she was a very small adult—but for a man who'd professed to having no interest in having children he was making an effort, and he wasn't looking too uncomfortable.

In fact, Mia could imagine all too well that with a bit of time Daniel might actually prove to be quite natural with his daughter. And that was something she would never have expected in a million years.

A ringing noise made Daniel pluck his phone from his pocket.

Lexi said imperiously, 'Me say hello.'

Daniel shook his head. 'Not this time, *chérie*.'

Mia went and picked Lexi up and Daniel stood too, answering his phone and speaking in rapid-fire French, too fast for her to grasp everything. He was frowning when he terminated the conversation. Mia had understood enough to know it affected her and Lexi.

'What is it?' she asked.

'The media interest is getting more intense.'

He went to the window and opened the shutters and looked out. Mia followed and gasped. The crowd of photographers had doubled.

'And this is before we've put a statement out.' Daniel sounded grim.

Mia felt panicky. 'It's going to get worse?'

Daniel nodded.

'What will we do? I can't stay in here all day every day. Lexi needs to get out and run around.'

'There's only one solution.'

Mia was sure she wasn't going to like this. 'What solution?'

'You and Lexi will have to move in with me until things die down a bit. I can protect you both better there.'

CHAPTER FIVE

MIA HAD PUT up a fight, but it had been weak and short-lived. She'd had no defence. Not with that baying mob outside. She couldn't subject her daughter to all that attention and potential danger.

Within hours Daniel had assembled a team of people who had come and helped Mia to pack what they needed. He'd also told her to write a list of things they required for Lexi and given it to another assistant.

They'd gone out through a side entrance and slipped into Daniel's car before any photographers had noticed.

And now they were in the hushed and exclusive confines of Daniel's apartment at Place Vendôme. The place was even more intimidating in the daylight. It looked vast. And also, more worryingly, very child-unfriendly. Especially for a toddler who had a mind of her own and could disappear faster than snow on a hot stone.

'What is it?' Daniel asked. He must have seen something on her face.

Mia looked around with Lexi in her arms. She was tired after all the unexpected activity over the past few hours and her head rested on Mia's shoulder, her thumb in her mouth.

'It's just…not really designed for a small person.'

Daniel frowned. Then his eyes drifted to Lexi and understanding dawned. 'Of course. Tell me what we need to do.'

Mia's chest tightened at the use of the word *we*. All her life the only *we* had been her and her mom, and her and Lexi. But now it was different. A feeling of vulnerability swept over her again. She didn't like it. She felt exposed. Out of control.

'Short of redesigning the whole apartment?' she said, half joking. 'For a start it needs to be made child-proof. Sharp edges are out—she's low to the ground and prone to falling over a lot. And we need a play area. She can sleep in my room. But first she needs to eat.'

The butler appeared and Daniel said, 'Go with Paul to the kitchen and talk to the chef. He can make what-ever you need.'

Her head still spinning at the speed with which their lives had been turned upside down, Mia dutifully fol-lowed Paul to the kitchen—a vast, gleaming space full of state-of-the-art equipment with an elegant dining area. There was no highchair yet, but the friendly chef made something simple for Lexi and she sat on Mia's lap while she fed her.

After that Mia sensed Lexi was approaching being overtired and would come perilously close to having a small meltdown if she didn't get some rest. But no way was she going to go down while everything around them was so different. The little girl was torn between exhaustion and wanting to explore.

Mia found Daniel in his study, a bright room full of bookshelves and a massive desk with three computers. He stood up when she came in and her arms tightened reflexively around Lexi.

'I need to take her out for a walk. She'll sleep in her stroller. I could do with some fresh air too.'

'I'd go with you, but I can't at the moment. I've got some people coming shortly, to have a look at the apartment and see what they can do to make it as safe as possible.'

The power of unlimited funds. It made Mia think of the small trailer where she'd grown up with her hard-working mother. She'd been constantly bruised from hitting the edges of tables and doors.

'Okay, thank you.'

Daniel followed her out of his study. 'You won't be alone, though. I've got security standing by in case you wanted to go out.'

Mia looked at Daniel. 'That's a bit over the top, isn't it?'

'You're not going without Security and that's non-negotiable.'

Once again she knew it was futile to argue.

Mia bundled Lexi up in her coat and they went downstairs, where the stroller was waiting with a burly man called Pierre. He said, 'Don't worry about where I am. You just go where you want.'

They went out through a back entrance which led into an enchanting landscaped private garden, and then another entrance out to a side street. Mia sucked in the cool autumn air gratefully. They walked out to Rue de Rivoli and across it to the Jardins des Tuileries, another of the city's most famous and beautiful parks.

Mia let Lexi out in one of the playgrounds and couldn't stop a smile at her daughter's carefree joy. Another pang of guilt gripped her, knowing she'd kept this from Daniel.

He could have easily thrown her to the lions today and left her to fend for herself with the press. There were plenty of men who would deny paternity until proved and try to wriggle out of responsibility. But he had stepped up without question. And he'd accepted Lexi on sight—which made her wonder about his sister and what she'd been like.

When Lexi got bored with the swings and slide, Mia took her back to the apartment. There were already a couple of trucks parked outside and delivery men carrying boxes inside.

When she got up to the apartment she saw nothing much changed at first, but then she noticed that the sharp edges of the tables were covered in thick pieces of foam. Also, some smaller tables and *objets d'art* had been removed.

Paul appeared in the doorway and said, 'Let me show you to your suite of rooms, Ms Forde.'

Mia checked Lexi quickly. She had fallen asleep in the stroller, so she put a blanket over her and left her, having learnt from previous experience to make the most of these snatched moments.

She followed Paul, saying, 'Please, call me Mia. I don't stand on ceremony.'

He inclined his head and then led her further into

the apartment, down a thickly carpeted hall to a door at the end. When Mia went inside it was hard not to let her jaw drop. There was a massive bedroom with a four-poster bed. An en suite bathroom led to a dressing room. And then, back in the bedroom, Paul opened a door that was cleverly designed to match the wallpaper into a smaller anteroom.

'Mr Devilliers is suggesting that this could be a good room for the nursery?'

A fluttery bird of panic beat at Mia's chest. 'Thank you, but Lexi's cot can go in the bedroom. We won't be here for too long, so there's no point going to all the trouble of setting up a nursery.'

'As you wish. The cot should be set up within the hour.'

Back in the main part of the apartment Lexi hadn't moved, still deeply asleep. Mia placed another light blanket over the hood of the stroller, creating a kind of cocoon.

She went over to the window and looked out. Her thoughts flew to the future when, once access arrangements had been made, Lexi would inevitably have a room and a life here of her own, without Mia. It made her feel hollow inside. Because now more than ever she had to come to terms with the fact that those very deeply secret dreams she'd once had of having a happy family would never come true.

She'd allowed herself to fantasise about it with her first boyfriend. He'd told her he respected her. He'd told her he loved her. And she'd been so grief-stricken after her mother's death, and desperate for connection, that she'd believed in him and his words and she'd projected her fantasy onto a relationship that had been a cruel lie.

It was only after he'd humiliated her and exposed her dreams for the fantasy they were that she'd realised how desperate she'd been to believe in a fairy tale. And that she'd never really loved him.

But she hadn't realised that bit until she'd met Daniel and—

'Where's Lexi?'

Mia whirled around. Her jaw felt tight from thinking of the past. She relaxed it.

She pointed towards the stroller in the corner. 'She's asleep...worn out after all the activity.'

'And you? Are you okay?'

There was a flutter near Mia's heart. She crushed it. Never more than right now did she need to remember the past and the lessons she'd learnt.

'I'm fine. I didn't say thank you for taking us in. I don't know what we would have done if—'

Daniel waved a hand. 'It's nothing. I was hardly going to leave you defenceless. Lexi is my daughter.' Then he said, 'There's something you should know.'

'What?'

'I've put out a statement to quell the media interest, but I've added a piece at the end.'

Mia looked at Daniel. 'What, specifically?'

He walked over and handed her his phone. She took it and looked at the screen, where there was a press release. It said:

Daniel Devilliers and Mia Forde are very pleased to announce that they have a child from a previous brief relationship and that they are happily reunited. They ask for privacy at this time. Thank you.

Mia's jaw went slack. She almost dropped the phone. She looked up as Daniel took it out of her hand. She tried to make her mouth work, but nothing came out.

She tried again. 'Happily reunited?'

A dull roaring was building in her head. Daniel had manoeuvred her and Lexi with such skill and ease...

Words spilled out. 'I actually gave you the benefit of the doubt when you said you hadn't tipped off the press.'

'I didn't.'

Daniel kept his voice low, mindful of the sleeping child.

Mia started to pace in front of him, and that drew his eye to her tall body. She was wearing a long button-down dress. Dark red with golden flowers. A belt around her slim waist. The buttons were open low enough that he could see the tantalising vee of her cleavage. She wore that battered leather jacket she seemed to love so much.

Soft, flat ankle boots gave the whole look an effortlessly chic and bohemian élan. He remembered that she'd always been self-conscious about her sense of style, or what she saw as her lack of style. But she had style in spades.

Her hair was down. She wore practically no make-up. It reminded him of the first time he'd seen her at that photoshoot. She'd reminded him of a lioness, with her green eyes and wild hair. She resembled a caged lioness right now.

She didn't seem to have heard him. 'I can't believe I trusted you enough to let you do this to us—'

'Mia.'

She stopped. Looked at him.

He said, 'I didn't tip off the press and I added the piece about being reunited at the last minute because it will be the most expeditious way of getting the press off our backs.'

She put her hands on her hips. 'How, exactly?'

Daniel curbed the urge to cover her mouth with his until all that spikiness was turned into passion.

'Because,' he said, 'if the press thinks we're back together they'll be interested for a while but they'll soon grow bored. But if you're here and we're not a couple they'll hound us until they find out more.'

Mia looked suspicious. 'Lexi and I could stay some-where else.'

'It'll be exactly the same as it was at your apart-ment. I can provide better protection here.'

Mia started to pace again. Eventually she stopped. Bit her lip. And then said grudgingly, 'I guess I can see some logic in that.'

She folded her arms, and Daniel had to grit his jaw against the urge to drop his gaze to where he could already imagine the swells of her lush breasts. *Dieu.* He was no better than a schoolboy.

'But how long exactly does this charade have to go on before they lose interest? A week? Two?'

Daniel saw the trepidation on her face. The sense of things being out of her control. And he almost felt sorry for her. Until he remembered that she'd kept his child from him for eighteen months. Lexi was a rapidly forming little human being, with spades of personality, and up until now she'd had no father figure.

That reminder firmed his resolve. 'For as long as it takes for this story to no longer be a liability.'

'But...that could take weeks.'

Daniel shrugged, trying not to let Mia's huge green eyes affect him. Eyes big enough to drown in. Eyes that had captured him from the moment he'd seen her.

'I doubt it,' he said. 'There's bound to be another story that takes precedence. They'll move on.'

'But right now they think that we're a couple.'

'Yes. And to that end I propose we take the heat out of the story by appearing in public together as soon as possible.'

She was suspicious again. 'What do you mean *as soon as possible*?'

'This evening.'

The colour faded from Mia's face. 'This evening?' Her voice was a squeak. He remembered how reluctant she'd been to appear with him in public before—in his world—and how he'd found it refreshing after being with women who had maximised their relationship with him to improve their own social profile.

But Mia had never wanted that kind of exposure. In spite of the fact that she would have got a lot out of it professionally to be seen on his arm. At the time he hadn't looked too deeply into her reasons for why that might be, but now... Now he cursed his lack of foresight.

It hadn't mattered before, because they'd broken

up and no one had been much the wiser, but this was very different.

'We should talk before we appear together,' he said.

'About what?'

'About why you were always so averse to being seen with me in public. If you have any skeletons in your closet you need to tell me now, Mia, because they *will* find them.'

'If you have any skeletons...'

Mia felt claustrophobic. She needed air. She instinctively moved towards the windows and opened them, stepping out onto the small balcony outside.

Within seconds she heard shouting from the square below and looked down to see people—mostly men, as far as she could make out—with cameras in their hands, tilting them up towards where she stood.

She hadn't even fully grasped who they were or what they were doing until two big hands went to her waist, pulling her back inside. Daniel closed the window again and faced her. Mia felt a little shaky, but she feared it was more from the imprint of his hands on her than the photographers.

'Those were—'

'The same paparazzi. They've followed you here.'

Mia felt hot. Constricted. Daniel held out a hand. 'Here, give me your jacket. I'll get you some water.'

Mia shrugged off her jacket and handed it over. Daniel went to the drinks cabinet and Mia checked on Lexi, trying to gather her wits as she did so. Lexi was still out for the count. It wouldn't make for a pretty night later, but right now Mia was willing to bend the rules.

It was all hitting home—just how much their lives had changed and were going to change further. On some level she'd known this, but she'd been blocking it out. Like a coward. She had never expected Daniel to say that they were a couple again, though.

And yet she couldn't deny that the logic behind it did make sense. She'd seen how some other more high-profile models had been sucked into the maelstrom of various scandals, and she'd always thanked her lucky stars she wasn't at that level of fame.

But now she *was* the one in the headlines, and Daniel was obviously realising that she was a potential liability.

'Mia—'

'I wasn't—'

They spoke at the same time. Mia accepted the glass of water Daniel offered, took a breath and said, 'I wasn't averse to being seen with you because I was afraid of press attention. I have nothing to hide…not really. Beyond growing up with a single parent in a trailer park in the shabbier end of Monterey, California.'

'You never spoke of your father. Is he around?'

They hadn't spoken of him because Mia had been deliberately keeping Daniel at arm's length last time. But now she knew she had no choice. And if she had a skeleton this was it. Mia put the glass down on a nearby table.

'The truth is that I don't know who he is.'

Daniel frowned. 'How is that possible?'

'I know that might be hard to understand, when you

come from a world where you can date your ancestors back to the dawn of time.' Mia's voice was tinged with bitterness.

Daniel's eyes flashed pewter and his jaw clenched.

Before he could say anything Mia held up a hand. 'I'm sorry, that wasn't fair.' She lowered her hand. 'The truth is that my mother always clammed up whenever I asked her about him. She never gave me a name. Didn't want to talk about him. Ever. It was only after she died that an old friend of hers told me that my mom went to a party after high school graduation. She was drugged and woke up the next morning dishevelled. Not feeling well. Sore. She fell pregnant as a consequence of that night. Her friend told her she should go to the police, tell them that something had happened to her, but my mom was so ashamed that she wouldn't. Her parents were strict, religious. They would have thrown her out. She moved to California and had me, and brought me up by herself.'

Mia looked at Daniel, expecting to see disgust or horror. But there was an expression she couldn't read on his face. He said, 'I'm sorry. That can't have been easy. For her or for you.'

Mia shrugged. 'I didn't know anything else, and she was a good mother. She made up for the lack of a father.'

Until she'd died, and Mia had felt so unmoored that she'd blindly sought out the first port in a grief-stricken storm.

'Is there a chance your father knows about you?'

'I guess…whoever he is…he might have heard something… But, given the circumstances, I don't think he'll be coming forward, do you?'

The bitterness in Mia's voice was hard to hide. She wasn't responsible for her parents' actions, but she'd always felt a little tainted by what her father had done. How he had violated her mother.

'That still doesn't explain why you were always so reluctant to step into my world with me. What was that about, if not fear of the press?'

Mia went cold.

No way was she going to tell Daniel about her ultimate humiliation.

She avoided his eye and shrugged minutely. 'You were—*are*—rich and powerful. I just had no interest in that world. It was that simple.'

Daniel made a snorting sound. 'Things are rarely that simple. It was more than mere lack of interest, Mia.'

Damn him. She glared at him. 'It's really none of your business and it has no bearing on anything now.'

Daniel leaned against the back of a couch and crossed one ankle over the other. 'Now I'm really intrigued.'

Mia wanted to stamp her foot. She recognised the obstinate expression on Daniel's face all too well. He would push and probe until she gave up all her secrets.

'Fine. If you must know, it was my first boyfriend. He was rich. Very rich. He came from a family that could date itself back to the *Mayflower*. I worked as a waitress in the local country club and he saw me there…and seduced me. Then he dumped me. It turned out the only reason he'd spoken to me was to get me into bed. He never intended on having a relationship with me because I was, in his words, *"trailer trash"*.

He led me to believe that he wanted me in his world, that he was prepared to introduce me to his family, while at the same time he was getting ready to announce his engagement to a far more suitable woman. The worst thing was that I fell for it. It wasn't long after my mom had died and he offered a sense of connection. I thought I wanted to be accepted by him and his world.'

'Are you saying I reminded you of him?' Daniel's voice was like steel.

Mia swallowed. She couldn't in all honesty say that, because at no point had Daniel ever reminded her of *him*. But he had stirred up enough powerful emotions and sensations to make her scared enough to keep him at arm's length.

'No, you're nothing like him. He was a coward. I'm ashamed to admit I allowed him to—'

Daniel stood up and shook his head, cutting her off. 'No, don't say it. He took advantage of you, Mia. He saw a beautiful young woman, and maybe a chink of vulnerability, and exploited it.'

Mia hated the emotion that climbed up her chest at Daniel's perspicacity.

'Is he also the reason why you don't like gifts of jewellery?'

She nodded. 'He gave me what he told me was a diamond necklace, but it was just cubic zirconia. All part of the act to make me think he wanted more than sex.'

Daniel said a rude word in French. To Mia's surprise, she didn't feel exposed or newly humiliated after telling Daniel—she felt vindicated. Lighter. But then she'd never told anyone else what had happened to her, and to realise that it was Daniel she'd just confided in… *Now* she felt exposed.

Suddenly eager to move on from the past, Mia asked, 'This evening…where are we going?'

'It's the Paris Ballet's gala night at the Palais Garnier.'

Mia was immediately intimidated at the thought of the stunning Paris *opéra* building. It was one of the most iconic landmarks of Paris and she'd never been inside.

'But I couldn't possibly go—what about Lexi?'

'Paul's daughter works as a nanny but she's between jobs at the moment. She can babysit.'

'That's convenient.' In Daniel's world, everything fell into place. Mia shouldn't have forgotten that. She said, 'I'm not going anywhere until I meet her and feel that I can trust her with Lexi.'

'Of course. I've arranged for her to come in an hour—that should give you plenty of time to see how you feel about her and see how she interacts with Lexi.' Daniel looked at his watch. 'I have to take some calls in my study. You'll find a range of dresses for this evening in your dressing room. It's a black-tie event.'

He was turning to go and, feeling claustrophobic again, Mia said, 'That's *if* I go.'

The tiniest of smiles played around the corner of Daniel's mouth, making Mia remember how it had felt to be kissed by him. All-consuming. Drugging. Addictive. She'd never forgotten.

She half expected him to say something smart, arrogant, but all he did say was, 'Of course. Only if you feel comfortable enough to leave Lexi for a few hours.'

He turned and left and Mia felt curiously deflated.

There was a sound and movement from the stroller in the corner. Lexi was waking up. Mia welcomed the distraction—anything to avoid thinking about their new situation and the very real possibility that she would be appearing in public in a few hours on Daniel Devilliers' arm.

'She's adorable.'

Mia smiled at the woman, who was just a year or two younger than her. They were sitting cross-legged on the floor of Lexi's new playroom, watching the toddler wreak happy havoc around her. 'She likes you.'

Lexi was besotted with her 'new friend' Odile, Paul's daughter. The young woman was clearly experienced, and had already managed a mini meltdown with an equanimity that had given Lexi no alternative but to calm down.

Much to Mia's chagrin, it wasn't looking as if she'd have an excuse to duck out of accompanying Daniel to this event. Nevertheless, she said a little hopefully, 'Are you sure it's not putting you out to babysit at such short notice?'

Odile smiled. 'Not at all. To be honest, I'm saving to go travelling next year, so every extra euro helps.'

Mia knew what that was like. She'd scrimped and saved to fly to Europe to further her modelling career and see something of the world. The fact that she'd got no further than France was a twist she hadn't expected, but when she looked at Lexi now her heart swelled with so much love she couldn't regret anything.

A shadow darkened the doorway and Mia looked up to see Daniel.

Lexi toddled over. 'Hi, Man! Play!'

Daniel smiled and Mia's heart hitched.

'Not right now, *mignonne*. I need to speak to your Mama.'

Odile expertly distracted Lexi and led her over to look at some toys. Mia stood up and went out of the room, closing the door behind her.

Daniel lifted a brow. 'Well?'

Mia sighed. 'She's perfect. Lexi loves her.'

'Okay, then, we leave in an hour.'

Mia wished she could avoid this, but she couldn't. He was Lexi's father, and if she wanted some kind of order restored in their lives she would have to go along with his plan. For now.

The strapless dress was ice-blue. It was low-cut enough to make Mia want to tug the fabric over her breasts, but the other dresses hadn't been much more discreet. The material hugged her torso just under her breasts, and then fell in soft swathes of material to the floor. It was elegant and romantic.

She'd managed to tame her hair back into a rough chignon, and she'd applied a little more make-up than she'd normally wear, using it like a tool that might give her some sort of illusion that she was working and not playing herself.

The thought of appearing in front of the world's press on Daniel's arm was intimidating, but it also touched on a very secret part of her where she'd once allowed herself to dream that possibly her relationship with Daniel *was* different from the experience she'd had before, and that perhaps she could allow herself to let him bring her into his world gradually, until she built up her trust again.

But then she'd seen the article in the paper about his 'arrangement, not engagement'. Just in time—before she'd made a complete fool of herself. Again.

Her reaction to the article had exposed her enough. This time she was prepared. Under no illusions. Daniel could not hurt her again.

Mia shut down her circling thoughts. Slipping her feet into high-heeled silver sandals and doing them up, she gave herself a last once-over and picked up the clutch and matching cape.

Daniel was finding it hard to keep himself from mentally undressing Mia. There was a discreet slit in her dress and a tantalising length of toned golden thigh, tempting him to place his hand there and move it higher, to the apex between her legs where he would feel the throbbing heat at the centre of her body.

He shifted in the back seat of the car, his own body throbbing in response. She'd taken his breath away when she'd walked into the reception room a short while before. He'd seen her transformed before, from her more casual aesthetic into something far more sleek when she was working—but he'd never seen her transformed for *him*. For a date.

Other women had. But not Mia. Because everything about being with her had been different. Challenging. She'd made him work to be with her. But it had been worth it—and not just on a carnal level. That had been the most surprising thing.

Mia turned to look at him now and her scent tickled his nostrils, light and fresh but with a musky base. Not unlike her. His first impression of her had been that she was sunny and carefree, but as he'd got to know her she'd shown more complex layers.

She said, 'I'm not wearing any jewellery. Will that be an issue?'

When Daniel had first seen her in the dress he'd automatically known that diamonds would show it, and her, off to their best advantage. And he'd known exactly which ones.

He looked at her. 'You wouldn't mind wearing it?'

She avoided his eye and he felt a physical surge of anger again at the thought of what her so-called boyfriend had done to her. *Trailer trash.*

'It wasn't the jewellery I had an issue with, it was the gift. I didn't want to be made a fool of again.'

Unable to help himself, Daniel reached out and touched Mia's jaw, making her turn her face towards him. 'He was the fool, Mia. Never you.'

He saw her throat work as she swallowed. Saw the flare of emotion in her eyes making them brighter green.

'You don't need to say that.'

The urge to kiss her in that moment was huge. Daniel almost shook with the effort it took not to tug her close. But they were pulling up outside the majestic Palais Garnier now, so Daniel reluctantly took his hand down and said, 'We're here.'

CHAPTER SIX

MIA'S FINGERS TIGHTENED around Daniel's hand as they stood at the bottom of the steps leading up to the majestic entrance. He shot her a look. She gave an imperceptible nod to say she was ready, when she was anything but.

They walked up the steps that were overlaid with a red carpet. Mia was very aware of Daniel's physicality next to her, oozing Alpha male energy. His bespoke classic black tuxedo fitted like a second skin, enhancing his lean strength. She'd been blisteringly aware of him in the back of the car beside her, and she was still breathless from the way he'd touched her and looked at her. From what he'd said.

'He was the fool.'

It hadn't meant anything. Not really. She had to get her desire and her rampant imagination under control. If he suspected she still wanted him she would literally have no dignity left.

People were turning to look at them. Eyes widened when they recognised who Daniel was. Then slid to her. Instinctively Mia lifted her chin. And then the paparazzi spotted them. But this time she was prepared, and she felt herself automatically slipping into work mode, so she could pretend this was just a photo shoot and counteract the intimidation she felt.

When they reached the entrance Daniel stopped. Mia looked up at him, hoping that he couldn't see the effect he was having on her. And then, before she could say or do anything, he was sliding an arm around her waist and pulling her into him.

It all happened too quickly for her to put up her guard, especially when she still felt a little raw after his words and the way he'd looked at her in the car. She couldn't fight the helpless temptation to go with the flow of her blood—which was towards Daniel. To get closer. With his free hand, he tipped up her chin. All she could see were those grey eyes.

The emotions he aroused were fading into the background to be replaced with pure physicality. She craved to have his mouth on hers with a hunger that blotted everything else out. All concerns. Without even being aware of it, her hand found and curled around the lapel of his jacket, as if to stop him pulling away.

It had been like this between them from that first day they'd met. Instant heat. An urgency.

And then Daniel's mouth was on hers and a deep sigh moved through Mia. The past fell away. There was only this moment and the familiar firm contours of his mouth, enticing her to open up to him, to take the kiss deeper. She did it without thinking, acting instinctively. It was as if they'd kissed only yesterday, and also as if it had been a thousand years ago. Both achingly familiar and new again. His tongue touching hers lit a fuse that connected directly to the pulse of heat between her legs.

But then Daniel was pulling back, taking his mouth off hers. Mia heard the sound of people around her, the outside world slowly breaking through the heat haze in her brain. And with the sounds came the crash of reality.

Her eyes snapped open. Daniel was looking down at her with no discernible expression on his face.

The full impact of what she'd just allowed to happen—enthusiastically participated in—hit her like a body-blow.

Daniel's arm was still around her waist. She pushed against his chest, when a moment ago she'd been pulling him closer.

'What was that in aid of?' *Bit late for outrage now*, jeered a voice in Mia's head.

'We're meant to be reunited, remember? The object of this evening is to convince people that there's really no story.'

Mia was aware of pops of light coming from the direction of the photographers. Self-consciousness crawled up her spine. Daniel had known what he was doing. He'd executed a perfectly clinical kiss for the cameras. And it was too late for her to act blasé.

She pulled away and Daniel's arm slackened enough to let her step back. 'Next time,' she said, 'do me the courtesy of asking first.'

She turned and stalked ahead of him into the building. Not even the sight of the grand marble staircase and the lavish Baroque-inspired interior could distract her from the fact that even if he'd asked her permission she still would have said yes.

* * *

Mia had been to plenty of glittering events before, but usually for work. Never like this, on someone's arm. And not just someone. A man everyone recognised on sight.

Daniel took her arm and gently guided her up to another level where there was a private drinks reception before the performance started. After someone had taken her cape Daniel handed her a glass of champagne.

Mia was more interested in the hors d'oeuvres. She hadn't had time to eat much while making sure that Lexi and Odile were going to be okay together. She tried to eat a concoction of caviar on the smallest piece of toast she'd ever seen, with as much grace as she could, but a steady stream of people were approaching Daniel, and he snaked an arm around her waist, pulling her into his side, effectively ruining her appetite for the evening.

One older, very well-preserved woman spoke to Daniel while barely glancing at Mia. She said, 'She's an American? You have a child with her? I hope this won't damage the brand, Mr Devilliers.'

Shocked at what she was hearing, and incensed that Lexi might be subjected to any kind of judgement, Mia cut in, 'Yes, I am American—and, yes we have a child. And I can assure you the Devilliers brand is quite safe.'

The woman looked at Mia as if she had two heads, and then she stalked off.

Mia looked at Daniel. 'Sorry, I couldn't help myself. Who was she?'

To Mia's surprise, Daniel's mouth quirked. 'One of the longest-serving members of the board.'

'Oh.'

'Your French is impeccable, by the way.'

Mia shrugged, self-conscious. 'I've had plenty of time to practise it over the last two years.'

Then she added tentatively, 'She looked angry... will this cause problems for you?'

Daniel took a sip of champagne, and even that relatively innocent movement made a skewer of desire arrow right to Mia's lower body.

'No. It's dinosaurs like her I'm trying to ease off the board. She and a few others are the only ones clinging onto the past. We have to move forward.'

At that point a melodic bell sounded to indicate that they needed to move into the theatre. Daniel took Mia's hand and led her out of the function room and along a corridor and into a private box.

Mia gasped when the full majesty of the auditorium was laid out before her. Tiers of seats rose up around the stage in a circle. The furnishings were lavish and totally over the top. Baroque. Dramatic. The ceiling was adorned with lush frescoes.

The crowd—most of whom had taken their seats— were as glittering as their surroundings. The men handsome in their tuxedoes.

'This is amazing,' she breathed as she sat down, momentarily distracted from everything else.

For a while, when she'd been younger, she'd had dreams of becoming a dancer. A teacher had even helped her apply for a grant to get into advanced classes, and Mia had had visions of going to Juilliard in New York. But one day she'd damaged her knee, and her dreams of becoming a dancer had turned to dust. And then, as if conspiring against her, her body had started to develop, giving her curves that would never have been acceptable in a ballet dancer.

So being here now was making her feel nostalgic and wistful. She had a sudden vision of an older Lexi, being brought here with her father to see a ballet performance, and emotion gripped her before she could stop it, stinging her eyes.

She cursed herself and kept her head averted from Daniel. Ever since she'd given birth to Lexi her emotions had sat just under her skin, and the most innocent and benign of incidents or things could set her off. Not to mention the tumult of being back in Daniel's orbit.

The lights went down and a hush fell over the crowd. Mia sat forward, her skin prickling with anticipation. Well, she told herself it was anticipation, and not because Daniel's tall, powerful body, his long legs stretched out before him, was close enough to touch. Smell.

She let the performance distract her from the man beside her, knowing it would be an all too brief respite…

A week after the ballet performance Mia spotted the floppy ear of Lexi's favourite bunny peeking out from under a couch and grabbed it. She looked around and saw the other detritus belonging to a small person. A cardigan shoved down between some cushions. A small shoe discarded by the door. And a sticky handprint on a glass coffee table.

She sighed. Already Lexi was treating this place like a small queen in her new domain, and even Mia had settled into the luxurious space far too easily. But she had to keep reminding herself that it was only temporary. And surely these transgressions into Daniel's pristine space would make him realise that having them here wasn't conducive to his newly acquired bachelor lifestyle?

That was if he was here to see them—which he wasn't. After the night at the ballet, which had left Mia feeling very emotional, Daniel had told her the following morning that he had to go to New York for a few days.

She'd schooled her expression while inwardly relishing the thought of a reprieve, to take stock of everything that had happened without Daniel's disturbing presence.

'Don't look so pleased,' he'd said dryly.

'What's in New York?' she'd asked.

'Our North American head office. We're having some discussions about a new campaign.'

'When will you be back?' Mia had asked nonchalantly.

'Before the weekend.'

But it was Friday night now, and he was not back. He was still in Manhattan on business. Not that Mia had any jurisdiction over him, so she shouldn't even be wondering about it, or feeling a disturbing pang of disappointment.

He'd called a couple of times during the week, mainly to ask about Lexi. He'd asked that Mia send him videos of Lexi every day and she had, feeling a very disturbing glow of warmth in her chest at his interest in his daughter.

During their conversation on Wednesday night he'd commented, 'You were working today?'

Mia had immediately felt defensive. 'Yes, it was a small job, booked in before…all this. Odile came with me and brought Lexi.'

'It wasn't a criticism, Mia. I know you work.'

She'd relaxed marginally and said dryly, 'Actually, my agent told me today that she's never had so many calls asking about my availability. It would appear my stock has risen all of a sudden.'

'You know you're not under pressure to work, Mia,' Daniel had responded. 'You don't have to worry about money.'

She'd tensed. 'I support myself, Daniel. I always have and I always will. We don't need—'

'You're the mother of my child,' Daniel had cut in, and then muttered something under his breath about her being stubborn. 'Lexi is now my responsibility too. You can work and save all you want, but you're not her sole provider any more.'

Mia had bitten her lip. Of course she wouldn't deprive her child of support from her father, but after that call she'd wondered how it would work—Lexi living a life of luxury with her *papa* and then coming back to a much more modest existence with her mother.

Now, feeling the onset of a headache, Mia was picking up Lexi's discarded items when she heard her mobile phone ringing and plucked it out of the back pocket of her jeans.

Daniel.

She answered, her voice sounding unaccountably husky. 'Hi.'

'Hi,' Daniel replied.

He sounded a little tired, and Mia had a mental image of him loosening his tie. Sitting back in a big chair. The skyline of Manhattan behind him. Because surely he must be in one of those sky-skimming buildings with a jaw-dropping view?

Mia perched on the edge of a couch. The apartment was dimly lit. It somehow felt more intimate to have Daniel's voice in her ear through the phone than if he was here himself.

He said, 'I'm sorry I didn't make it back before the weekend.'

Something fluttered in Mia's chest. She crushed it. 'That's okay. You don't have to explain your movements, Daniel.'

There was a dry tone in his voice. 'You're not my roommate, Mia. You're the mother of my daughter.'

Mia scowled into the phone.

Then Daniel said, 'Actually, my plans have changed.'

'Oh?'

'Are your and Lexi's passports up to date?'

As it happened, Mia had had to renew her passport recently, so she'd ordered Lexi's first passport too.

'Yes...' she answered cautiously, with no idea where this was going.

'Good. I have to fly to Costa Rica tomorrow for a week, to oversee a shoot. I'd like you and Lexi to join me. You'll fly out tomorrow on a private plane. Odile is free to travel with you, to help take care of Lexi. I've already spoken to her to check.'

Mia's mouth dropped open in shock, but before she could say anything or object Daniel spoke again.

'To save us all some time, I'll explain why it's a good idea. With all of us being absent from Paris for a while, it'll speed up the process of the press losing interest. By the time we return they'll have moved on. We'll be old news.'

Mia's mouth closed. Then opened it again. 'So by the time we return Lexi and I can return to our apartment?'

For a moment Daniel said nothing, and then, 'It'll certainly make it much more likely.'

She knew he was right. If they weren't here, there was no story. She'd noticed paparazzi in the park these last few days, even though the security presence had kept them back. But she didn't like exposing Lexi to their lenses. So any method of minimising that had to be a good thing.

She said, 'Okay, then.'

Daniel was brisk. 'Good. I'll have my assistant come and help you pack in the morning. She'll arrange transport to the airport, and anything else you might require for Lexi. Odile will meet you at the plane. See you in Costa Rica, Mia.'

Mia was tempted to change her mind at the last minute, but Daniel had terminated the connection.

Too late.

She wondered if she was completely delusional for

thinking for a second that it was a good idea to go to a tropical paradise with the most disturbing man she'd ever met.

The following day, after a twelve-hour flight and then a shorter hop from San José to Santa Teresa on the Nicoya Peninsula, Mia and Lexi and Odile were in… paradise. That was the only way to describe it.

The air was warm, inviting Mia to melt and relax and forget all her worries and concerns. Like a siren call. The sun was setting over the Pacific Ocean in a glorious cascade of pinks and oranges and reds.

In front of where she stood, stupefied with awe, Mia could see people on a beach in the near distance, strolling, surfing… Dogs running alongside owners. Children playing. All against the backdrop of majestic surf. Behind them lay the lushest forest she'd ever seen. And in between these two things was this villa.

It was modern, but it sat in the tropical forest seamlessly. On several levels, it flowed down through the forest to a path which led to the beach, and it was truly breathtaking. Each level held a range of rooms, and at the top was a lounging/dining area, with an infinity pool that looked out over a canopy of trees to the ocean and the vast sky.

The lower levels held bedrooms and a gym and media centre. Also a room that looked like an office. From all these rooms the ocean was visible through a lush tangle of forest. And from this lowest level there was a private path to the beach.

But even in spite of all these distractions the back of her neck prickled just before she heard Daniel say from behind them, 'Sorry I wasn't here when you arrived. The preparation meeting for the shoot ran over.'

Mia braced herself before turning around. Lexi was sleepy in her arms. She hadn't slept much on the plane and now she was exhausted. But even bracing herself couldn't prepare Mia for the sight of a far more relaxed Daniel.

He was wearing a dark blue short-sleeved polo-shirt and linen trousers. His skin looked darker already. Shades covered his eyes. He looked cool and unbelievably suave. And masculine. The musculature of his chest was all too evident under the thin material of his top.

Mia immediately felt creased and gritty, in her long broderie anglaise dress and cream blazer.

Odile greeted Daniel and reached for Lexi, saying to Mia, 'I'll take Lexi up to the house and get her fed and ready to put down.'

Mia wanted to object, but Lexi was perfectly happy to be transferred to her new best friend Odile, and Mia knew she needed to go down before she tipped over into extreme over-tiredness.

She handed Lexi over as Daniel said thank you to Odile, and then, as Odile and Lexi made their way back up to the main part of the house, he pushed his shades onto his head and said to her, 'You met Gabriela?'

Mia nodded. 'She greeted us when we arrived and showed us around. She seems very nice.'

Daniel came and stood beside her. Mia tried not to feel self-conscious under that cool grey gaze. 'She is. She lives locally and her son maintains the property for me.'

Mia looked at him. 'You own this? It's not a rental?'

Daniel nodded. 'It's part of my portfolio, yes.'

Along with the family chateau outside Paris, and the apartment in New York, another in London, and undoubtedly more properties dotted around the world…

'How was Lexi on the journey?' Daniel asked.

Mia made a face. 'Okay…not great. Fractious. Her ears were sore.'

Daniel frowned. 'I never considered that.'

'People don't until they have children. That's why there are so many screeching babies on planes.'

'Will she be okay?'

Mia nodded. 'She'll be fine once she's been fed and put down. I'll go and make sure she's okay. Odile is exhausted too. She should have the rest of the evening and tomorrow off.'

'Of course. I have some calls to make, but I'll be eating in about an hour if you want to join me?'

The warm breeze caressed Mia's body. The sky was turning lavender now, and the smell of sea and sand and exotic blooms made the air fragrant. Night birds started their calls. And there was this man, as elemental as his surroundings in spite of the trappings of civilisation.

She could feel the pull to move closer, to have him envelop her in all that heat and steel. Transport her to an even more seductive paradise. It was dangerously romantic.

Mia stepped back before she made a fool of herself.

She shook her head. 'I'm quite tired myself, actually, I'll just grab something and then go to sleep with Lexi.'

Daniel watched Mia go, her flowing dress doing little to hide her long bare legs. She moved gracefully, her tawny hair trailing down her back and over her shoulders. For someone who'd just got off a transatlantic flight with a small child, she looked pretty perfect. In fact, she fitted into this wild landscape very well, with her naturally sun-kissed skin.

Daniel felt something ease inside him at the knowledge that they were here. It was a subtle shift. A sense that he could relax.

That thought registered and he scowled at himself—at the notion that Mia and Lexi's proximity was somehow beneficial for him.

Having Mia and Lexi here, far away from the French media and his conservative board—*that* was beneficial. As was the fact that he now had time to convince her of what he'd spent the last week realising was the only solution for them. The only solution he was prepared to accept.

Full commitment from Mia.

This wasn't what he had ever planned for his life, but the reality of having a daughter had aroused emotions and protective instincts he'd buried a long time ago with his sister. He wanted more for Lexi. He wanted to be able to nurture her and protect her. He'd failed his sister and he vowed now that he would not fail his daughter.

And, more selfishly, he wanted Mia back in his bed. For good.

* * *

The following day, after Mia had woken and fed Lexi and dressed her, she explored a little. There was no sign of Daniel, which brought her a mixture of relief and something else she refused to call disappointment. Gabriela told her he had gone to work—to wherever they were setting up the shoot.

Odile had gone into the pretty little town of Santa Teresa to explore. While passing through it yesterday Mia had thought it looked charming, and rustic. Full of cafés and artisan shops. Very bohemian. But she was happy to stay around the house and take Lexi to the beach to paddle in the surf, which delighted her. It was a long time, if ever, since they'd been able to relax like this.

In the afternoon, when Lexi didn't seem remotely inclined to go down for a nap, Mia dressed them both in swimwear and liberally applied a high-factor sunscreen.

To her surprise, when she'd explored more yesterday evening, she'd found the dressing room adjoining her very luxurious bedroom suite to be fully stocked with clothes. All in her size. When she'd mentioned it to Gabriela that morning the woman had told her that Daniel had instructed her to get a local boutique to deliver clothes for both her and Odile, and baby clothes for Lexi, in case they needed anything.

The fact that the clothes weren't a permanent fixture made Mia feel somewhat off-centre. She wondered if Daniel had ever kitted the dressing room out for anyone else. Surely he'd come here with lovers? It would almost be a crime not to—the place was so romantic and full of earthy sensuality.

But Mia quickly diverted her mind from that line of thinking. She didn't care if Daniel had been here with lovers. He could do what he liked with his properties.

She checked her reflection before they went out. She was wearing a one-piece swimsuit which had looked very conservative on the hanger, but it felt a lot more revealing now. One-shouldered, it had a cut-out above her hip, high-cut legs, and a top cut a little too low across her breasts for her liking.

But Lexi was grizzling now, and Daniel wasn't even here, so Mia told herself she was being ridiculous, plonked hats on their heads and went to the pool.

When Daniel rounded the corner of the building to walk onto the decked area by the pool he stopped in his tracks and his blood ran cold.

All he saw was Lexi in the pool.

He couldn't move. It was as if cement had been poured into his legs.

Helpless. Any minute now she was going to tip face-forward and—

'Hi, we weren't expecting to see you until later…'

Daniel's stricken gaze finally took in more detail. They were in the shallow end of the pool, and Mia had Lexi securely under the arms, holding her as she pulled her forward and back through the water. Lexi was splashing and babbling in baby language.

Not about to drown.

Not like his sister.

Mia must have seen something on his face. She stopped moving and said, 'Are you okay?'

Somehow Daniel managed to move forward, nearer the edge of the pool, but still at a distance. He hadn't considered this scenario.

He didn't answer Mia's question directly. He wished they would come out of the water. 'Shouldn't she have armbands?'

Mia smiled. 'She's a water baby. She's fine. I'm a qualified lifeguard, in any case.'

'Still, it's not safe. I should put something around the pool.'

Mia's eyes opened wide. 'It's fine, honestly. She won't ever be here unsupervised.'

She could be, though.

This was one of the reasons why he'd sworn never to have children. To avoid this crippling fear. That pool was a lethal accident waiting to happen—something Daniel never would have noticed before now, because to him it was merely an ornamental feature.

Mia said, 'It's probably time we came out now anyway. Lexi needs a wash and her dinner.'

She came up the steps out of the water with Lexi in her arms, and for the first time since he'd seen them in the pool the dread inside Daniel eased a little. The distraction of Mia in a swimsuit that clung like a second skin, leaving little to the imagination, helped too. Her hair was piled up on her head in a rough knot, showing off her spectacular bone structure and long neck. He seized on her beauty as something to cling to— something that brought him back from those awful tendrils of fear.

She came over to a lounger and wrapped Lexi in

a voluminous towel, rubbing her briskly and making her laugh.

The sound finally broke Daniel out of his stasis.

He went and sat on the other lounger and Lexi stretched out her arms towards him.

'Hi!'

Mia held on to her. 'She's all wet. She'll ruin your—'

Something swelled in Daniel's chest. Emotion and an instinct he couldn't ignore, part possessive and part fear. He plucked Lexi out of Mia's hands. 'It's fine.'

He'd held Lexi before, but he was surprised again at how solid she was. And trusting.

She immediately placed her hands on his face and declared, 'Hair face!'

Daniel smiled. He nuzzled his face against her cheek, making her squirm and giggle. When he looked at Mia he was surprised to see an arrested look on her face. Their eyes met and the expression disappeared as if he'd imagined it. An electric spark zinged between them. Her cheeks went pink.

She reached for Lexi again and he let her take her—but not before their fingers touched.

The colour in her cheeks deepened and Mia said, 'I should wash her off and prepare her dinner.'

She stood up, all long limbs and tantalising curves.

'Join me for dinner this evening,' Daniel said.

He could see her mouth open, could anticipate the refusal. But then she surprised him by saying, 'Okay. I'll join you once Lexi is down for the night.'

Mia looked at herself in the mirror. Her hair was curling wildly in the evening heat after her shower. Not much she could do about that. Anyway, it wasn't as if this was a date. She was having dinner with the father of her child, and they would stick to topics concerning only their daughter.

She'd chosen to wear a long kaftan-like dress which couldn't be remotely construed as sexy. But then, out of nowhere, an image popped into her head of Daniel with Lexi earlier, tickling her with his stubble, and suddenly Mia felt breathless.

She hated the tender part of her that it had affected. Seeing Lexi being held in his big hands. Protected. Safe. Already Lexi had experienced a more meaningful father-daughter relationship than Mia ever had.

Mia could also recall all too easily how Daniel's gaze had lingered on her body, making her blisteringly aware of the clinging wet swimsuit.

But she'd imagined the heat in Daniel's eyes. Must have. Projected her own desire on to him.

He didn't want her any more.

She'd never forget the way he'd looked at her that day when she'd told him she was pregnant. The shock. Horror. And then panic. And then later in the hospital, in the aftermath of her miscarriage, with a cold remoteness that had scared her.

After checking Lexi, and the baby monitor to make sure it was on, Mia went up to the next level, where they would eat.

When she saw where Gabriela had set the table she cursed silently. It was out on the terrace. The sky was dusky and gently flickering candles illuminated the space and the table. The scent of exotic blooms filled the air. It was all too seductive.

Daniel was standing at the rail that curved around

the terrace. He had his back to her and he was wearing a white shirt, sleeves rolled up, and dark trousers.

He turned around and the first thing Mia spotted was that his hair was damp and his jaw was clean-shaven. Need pierced her so acutely that she had to suck in a gasp.

Her hand tightened around the baby monitor.

He was holding a drink. 'What can I get you?'

Mia knew alcohol was the last thing she needed, but she needed the edges of her desire for Daniel blurred a little. 'A white wine, please.'

Daniel came back and handed her a cold glass.

Mia took a sip and relished the dry aromatic wine.

He lifted his glass, '*Santé*, Mia.'

She touched hers to his, avoiding his eyes like a coward. 'Cheers.'

She moved over to where he'd been standing. The lights of fishermen's boats were already visible, bobbing up and down in the sea. Presumably they were out because it was a calm evening.

She sensed Daniel coming to stand beside her. The little hairs stood up on her arms. 'It's so beautiful here,' she said.

'Yes, it is.'

'You must use it a lot. I would. I don't think I'd ever leave.'

'Actually... I don't use it as much as I'd like. I haven't been here now for a couple of years.'

Mia glanced at him. He'd put his back to the view and was leaning against the rail. Her mouth was open as she absorbed that nugget of information but she rapidly closed it.

Daniel's mouth quirked. 'I can practically hear your brain whirring. What are you thinking?'

A very timely discreet cough sounded from behind them, and Mia was relieved not to have to try and hide how much she wanted to know if he'd ever brought lovers here.

Gabriela had served up their starter—a deliciously light crab salad. Mia sat down and eyed the food with appreciation. But any hope that Daniel might not pursue the line of conversation turned to dust when he said, after a few minutes, 'You were going to say something, about me not coming here?'

Mia cursed him. She wiped at her mouth with a napkin and took a sip of wine. Then she forced herself to look him in the eye. 'It's so beautiful here—and private. I just thought that if you and your wife weren't… weren't sleeping together, it would be the perfect place to bring lovers.'

'Are you asking me if I took lovers during my marriage, Mia?'

Damn him, he was enjoying this.

She smiled sweetly. 'Never mind. It's none of my business.'

CHAPTER SEVEN

DANIEL WAS ENJOYING THIS. Watching Mia squirm.

'You're right, it's not your business. But, to sate your curiosity, no, I didn't. Nor did she. Sophie was conscious of the serious repercussions if she was found to be having an affair with a woman, and I… I respected her too much to risk it.'

Not to mention the fact that his libido at that time had flatlined.

He shifted in his chair as his now fully refunctioning libido made itself felt. Mia's hair was tumbling over her shoulders in wild abandon. She'd already acquired a golden glow to her skin, and freckles across her nose from the sun. The kaftan effectively covered her from neck to toe, but it was diaphanous enough to show tantalising glimpses of her perfect body.

Acting on an impulse, he found himself divulging, 'For what it's worth, I haven't ever brought a lover here.'

'Oh…'

Clearly she hadn't expected that.

Gabriela appeared then, to take the starter plates away and deliver the main course. A traditional Costa Rican beef and bean stew, light and tasty.

Daniel watched with interest as Mia tucked in. She'd never been shy about eating. He remembered staring at her the first time they'd gone for dinner, and she'd put down her fork.

'What? Is there something on my face?' she'd asked.

He'd commented dryly, 'I don't think I've ever seen a woman eat with so much relish.'

She'd blushed, and said a little tartly, 'It's a crime to waste good food.'

'I agree,' Daniel had said, beyond amused, and enthralled by her appetite and her defensiveness.

As if playing a cruel trick on him now, she looked up at him and swallowed her food before saying, 'What is it? Have I got something on my face?'

Daniel shook his head, not liking the swell of something in his chest. Something close to what he'd felt earlier when he'd played with Lexi.

Yet in spite of that unnamed emotion he found himself admitting, 'Actually, I haven't taken a lover since you.'

Mia's eyes went wide. Colour poured into her cheeks. She looked at him suspiciously. 'Did you just say—?'

He nodded, looking at her carefully. 'I haven't had a lover since you.'

She took a gulp of water.

'Have you?' he asked, suddenly feeling exposed.

He'd assumed she hadn't, because of Lexi, but maybe that had been naive. After her initial reticence Mia had been a voracious lover, and there was no reason for her not to have taken lovers in the interim.

The prospect sat like lead in his gut. But then she said, 'I…no. No, I haven't.'

A sense of satisfaction rushed through Daniel. He told himself it was satisfaction and not relief. She was avoiding his eye now. Her cheeks still flushed. Desire twisted in his gut.

Gabriela came out and took away the dinner plates, appearing oblivious to the crackling tension in the air. Mia suddenly appeared to be fidgety. She picked up the baby monitor and turned it on and off again, as if checking to make sure it was working.

Daniel said quietly, 'I haven't wanted another woman since you, Mia.'

Those huge green eyes met his. He saw her throat work. 'I… I can't say it's been the same for me.'

Daniel could see the pulse beating near the base of her throat. 'Liar.'

She sat up straight. Indignant. But no words came out. She left the baby monitor on the table and stood up and went over to the railing. Daniel followed her.

She said, 'I've moved on, Daniel. I've had a baby. I have more important priorities now.'

'You had *my* baby—which you kept a secret from me,' he pointed out. And then, 'And you might have different priorities, but you're still a desirable woman. Not just a mother. In case I haven't made myself completely clear, I still want you, Mia.'

Mia was reeling. *Daniel did want her.* She hadn't been imagining the heat between them. She hadn't been projecting her desire on to him.

As much as this made her feel somehow vindicated, it also terrified her. Because believing that Daniel didn't want her had enabled her to stay somewhat sane. Protected.

But now…if he knew how much she still wanted him…there would be nothing between them. Literally. No walls. No barriers. Nowhere to hide.

The fact that he hadn't slept with anyone since her was almost too much to try and comprehend. It stripped away her defences even more, leaving her dangerously exposed. Not helped by the all too seductive surroundings.

She turned to face him, feeling desperate, willing herself to say whatever it took to push him back. 'Look, Daniel, whatever was between us died the day our—'

He cut her off, his face taut. 'Do not say it.'

Mia swallowed her words, shocked at the stark tone in Daniel's voice. Shocked that she'd been willing to go so far as to remind them both of that awful day in the hospital.

He said now, 'I am sorry for how I reacted that day, but I can't go back and change it.'

Mia felt chastened. 'I know. I'm sorry too.' Especially now she knew why he'd reacted the way he had.

He said, 'Just because the relationship ended, it doesn't mean that our desire did. And if you're maintaining that it did then you're fooling no one but yourself.'

Still feeling desperate, she said, 'I don't want you any more.'

Daniel's eyes flashed.

Wrong thing to say.

She knew it as soon as his gaze narrowed on her mouth. 'You really expect me to believe that?'

Mia thought of the incendiary kiss that night at the ballet in Paris. Her cheeks burned, but she forced a shrug. 'Believe what you like, Daniel. I don't really care.'

He moved closer. Mia forced herself to stand firm, even though she could see the darkness of Daniel's chest under his shirt and smell his scent. Woodsy and musky and, oh, so masculine.

'Want to put it to the test, Mia?'

Mia quivered inwardly at that challenge. But she knew the only way to persuade Daniel that she didn't want him was to show him. He was a proud man. If he truly believed she didn't want him then he wouldn't push it.

She'd gone through a twenty-four-hour labour and given birth naturally—she could do this. Resist Daniel. Pretend that he didn't affect her.

She shrugged nonchalantly. 'Sure, knock yourself out.'

Mia fixed her gaze on a neutral spot just over Daniel's shoulder. But then he said, 'Close your eyes.'

Rolling her eyes a little first, Mia did as he asked, steeling herself not to react.

For a long moment Daniel did nothing. Mia cursed him. She desperately wanted to open her eyes, but didn't want to give him the satisfaction. But then the air shifted around her and she felt her hair being pulled over one shoulder.

He was behind her.

Every nerve-ending pulsed with awareness. She felt

his breath feather against her skin before his fingers pulled her kaftan away slightly, and then his mouth touched the spot between her neck and her shoulder.

He knew that was a sensitive spot for her. The fact that he'd even remembered—

The low-down, dirty...

Mia sucked in a breath when she felt Daniel's tongue touch her skin. Hot. Her hands gripped the railing. She refused to let him see an ounce of the battle she was fighting.

His hands—where were his hands? So far it was only his mouth on her skin, the tip of his tongue. Then it was gone.

Mia opened her eyes. She'd done it. She'd managed to withstand him.

She turned to go—but came face to face with Daniel's chest.

He tipped up her chin. Smiled. It was wicked. 'You didn't think you'd get away so easily, did you?'

Before Mia could formulate a response, and still just holding her chin with the lightest of touches, Daniel bent his head and covered her mouth with his, leaving her nowhere to hide.

It was an open-mouthed, explicit kiss. She opened her mouth to object, but somewhere in the moment of breathing in Daniel's essence and feeling his tongue touch hers in a bold move, she forgot why she wanted to.

Being surrounded by Daniel's heat and all that steely strength was an aphrodisiac that fatally scrambled every brain cell, until all she was aware of was that it wasn't enough. She wanted more. Needed total immersion.

She twined her arms around Daniel's neck, coming up on her tiptoes. Her breasts pressed against his hard chest. He shaped her waist, her upper back, hauling her closer. And then his hand was in her hair, fingers funneling deep, angling her head to take the kiss deeper, and his other hand found the curve of her bottom, caressing it through the thin material of the kaftan.

He pulled up her kaftan, baring her leg to the warm breeze. She felt his arousal press against her and moved instinctively against him. Like a needy little kitten. But still he didn't take his mouth off hers. His hand was on her bare bottom now, caressing. Fingers were sliding under the silk and lace of her underwear, coming close to where heat radiated out from the centre of her body.

Mia broke the kiss, pulled back. Vision blurry. She was breathing heavily. A few things sank in simultaneously—chief of which was that she'd withstood nothing. Proved nothing. Except that he was right.

Hot recrimination and something far more disturbing—sexual frustration—rose up inside her, giving her the strength to push back. Her kaftan fell down around her legs again.

Daniel was watching her with a neutral expression. She couldn't have borne it if he'd been smug.

At that moment a sound came from the baby monitor. *Lexi.* It jolted Mia back to reality.

She said to Daniel, even though she was aware that her dignity was in tatters, 'I didn't come here to be seduced by you.'

She walked back to the table on unsteady legs and picked up the baby monitor.

Daniel said from behind her, 'You can't deny this just happened and hide behind Lexi for ever.'

Mia fled.

Mia didn't sleep that night, and it had nothing to do with the heat and everything to do with that kiss, and Daniel's revelations, and the fact that he still wanted her. All together it was a powerful combination, and it left her feeling raw and gritty-eyed.

To her relief, the following morning Odile was more than happy to entertain Lexi, packing her up in the buggy and taking her for a stroll into the small town.

But then, instead of capitalising on her time off, Mia was restless. She walked down to the beach, but the surf looked too big to swim in, so she walked along the beach for a bit, and then back, trying not to consider what might happen between her and Daniel now.

If he properly set out to seduce her, as he had before, she didn't have a hope.

She saw a movement in her peripheral vision and looked to the tree line, where a path led back up to Daniel's house. Someone was waving at her. *Daniel.* Mia's heart skipped a beat. She was wearing a bikini top and shorts and felt too bare.

Daniel didn't come onto the beach. He waited till she was almost at the trees. He was wearing faded jeans and a white T-shirt, and he looked so ridiculously sexy that when he said to her, 'I need you,' she stumbled.

He reached out and caught her. And Mia thought to herself that if he kissed her right there, right now, she wouldn't be able to say no. She was almost trembling with the need rising in her body, and she knew she didn't have the strength to hide how he made her feel.

'Look, Daniel,' she said. 'What happened last night doesn't mean anything. I'm not interested in another affair—'

Daniel was shaking his head. 'I'm not talking about that.'

Now she felt foolish and exposed. But then she thought of something and went cold, her hands tightening on his arms. 'What is it? Is it Lexi?'

Daniel shook his head and tugged her further into the trees, away from the beach. 'Lexi is fine. Odile is giving her lunch right now.'

'Oh, okay…' Mia became aware of Daniel's very hard biceps under her hands. She took them down. 'What's up?'

Had she imagined him saying he needed her? She was losing it…

'We have a problem with the shoot. With the model, specifically.'

'Oh?'

'She developed pains in her abdomen last night and she's been taken to hospital. It looks like it could be appendicitis. She's being flown to San José today to get checked out. And that,' he continued, 'means we're now minus a model for the shoot.'

'I need you.'

Mia's eyes widened. 'You can't mean me. I don't have a high enough profile for one of your campaigns.'

'You'd be perfect. Trust me.'

Mia shook her head and started walking back up the path towards the house. 'We both know I'm not a

Devilliers model. I don't even know why I was cast for that first photoshoot.'

'Because I requested you.'

Shock made Mia stop and turn back to look at Daniel. Her heart thumped. 'You asked for me…specially? But you didn't even know me.'

'I saw you on a billboard. The picture where you're blowing a bubblegum bubble.'

Mia saw the image in her mind's eye. It had been an ad for a teen clothing line. Youthful and playful. Hence the bubblegum.

She shook her head. 'But that couldn't be further from the elegance and sophistication of Devilliers. What were you thinking?'

Daniel's eyes stayed hidden behind his shades. 'It was an instinctive thing. Your image resonated with a freshness I wanted to bring into Devilliers. Something less…reverent.'

She'd been less reverent, all right. They hadn't even styled her that day, and the photos that Daniel had asked her to pose for hadn't been used in the final campaign.

But, the knowledge he'd specifically asked for her made her feel even more vulnerable now. She said, 'It wouldn't take long for you to get another model here,' she said.

Daniel shook his head. 'This shoot is off the radar. It's something I want to present to the board as a fait accompli. I'm trying to move them in a more modern direction, and they're resistant to change, to say the least.'

Daniel had spoken of this before—his desire to haul

the company into the new century before it became known as just a legacy brand.

He said, 'If I have to book a new model now, the chances are they'll hear about it. They think I'm here on a personal holiday. With you and the baby.'

Mia felt silly for not realising he had an agenda. 'So it wasn't just to get us out of Paris and away from the media?'

Daniel shrugged. 'When you said you'd come, I made the best use of the situation to deflect their attention.'

Mia didn't know why she hadn't expected that. A man like Daniel was all about strategy. He took advantage of every angle.

'I…' She trailed off, realising she didn't have an excuse to say no.

'Please?' Daniel said.

Mia's mouth quirked. 'Now I *know* you're desperate.'

Daniel put a hand to his chest. 'You have such a low opinion of me.'

A delicate moment hung between them, reminiscent of the past and the very easy banter they used to have. Mia didn't have a low opinion of Daniel at all. In fact, from the moment they'd met he'd blasted through all her prejudices and confounded her expectations. He'd proved himself to be surprisingly humble for a titan of industry. He was arrogant, but never rude. More intelligent than anyone else she'd ever met. But he'd never used that intelligence to make someone—*her*—feel stupid, even if he had used to tease her for being a typical American with no appreciation for culture.

He'd hurt her, yes. Badly. But it was her fault. She'd let him in too deep. And there was no way she was going to let that happen again.

Mia folded her arms. 'I don't know if you can afford me.'

Daniel listed the fee they'd been paying the other model. Mia nearly fell backwards. This was another league.

She unfolded her arms. 'That sounds…reasonable.'

'You'll do it, then?'

Mia looked for a smirk or a hint of triumph on Daniel's face, but it was impassive. 'Okay. I don't see why not.'

In truth, Mia had never been good at relaxing. She preferred to be busy. So the thought of having something to do other than ruminate on memories or think about that kiss last night was all too welcome.

Except Daniel hadn't alluded at all to that kiss. In fact, he'd behaved as if nothing had happened. Maybe he was already regretting it and realising that pursuing Mia again wasn't worth it.

Which would be a *good* thing, she told herself now, as she followed Daniel back up to the house and tried to keep her gaze off his very taut backside.

A few hours later, Daniel was regretting his impetuous decision to ask Mia to fill in for the model. Not because she wasn't suitable for the job—the minute he'd seen her ready for the cameras he'd known that, actually, she was better than the original model—but because right now it was taking all his control and strength not to haul her away from the small crew, tear that skimpy swimsuit off her body and ease the throbbing ache that emanated from his groin to every part of his body.

Uncannily, he'd also realised at this moment that *she* had been the genesis for this very shoot—seeing her play around with the jewellery dressed in her jeans and T-shirt that first time he'd seen her had sparked something inside Daniel that was coming to fruition right here.

The whole concept was sexy decadence, which was a world apart from the refined elegance of most Devilliers campaigns, and that was why Daniel wanted to keep it top secret until he knew it would work.

The original model had certainly oozed a certain type of glamorous sexiness, but now Mia was elevating it to a level of sensuality that he knew the whole crew could feel. There was a buzz in the air that hadn't been there before.

The photographer—a woman—came up to Daniel during a change of set-up and held out her arm. She pointed to it, saying, 'Look, I've got goosebumps. Who *is* she? How come I've never seen her before? She's amazing, Daniel.'

'Yes, she is.'

He watched now as Mia stood up from where she'd been posing on her knees. An armed security guard came over and the stylist took off the jewellery Mia had been wearing for the last photos and placed it into a box he held. Another security guard watched over the rest of the jewellery on a nearby table. Together the collective value of jewels for this campaign was worth the debt of a small country.

Mia's deep-green-coloured swimsuit was a one-piece and perfectly modest; on anyone else. But not on her. The high-cut design made her legs look even longer, and the low-cut top edge drew the eye to her high, firm breasts.

Her skin glowed a darker shade of gold, thanks to a liberal application of false tan, and her hair was slicked back. The make-up was cutting edge. Red lips dominated her flawless face. Her eyes were huge.

The whole effect was a little lurid to the naked eye, but it was showing up on camera exactly the way Daniel and the team had envisaged—a very rich, colour-saturated, high-glamour decadent feel.

This was the backdrop for the stunning jewels that Mia was modelling. Bold, simple designs featuring big gemstones set in different metals. Silver, rose-gold, gold, platinum. It was luxe and very modern, framed perfectly by the lush green forest they were shooting in.

An assistant handed a wrap to Mia, who pulled it on. She slipped on flip-flops and came over to Daniel. 'Can I borrow your phone to call Odile and check on Lexi?'

Daniel pulled his phone out of his pocket, dialled a number. 'Here.'

Mia walked away with the phone held out. It was a video call, and he heard Lexi's excited, 'Mama!' followed by some unintelligible babble.

And then he heard Mia say, 'Really? Wow!'

He couldn't help but compare Mia's obvious love and care for her daughter with his own mother's distinct lack of care—and his father's. He could never recall his mother talking to him with that loving tone of voice. It had always been cold. Or dismissive. Or irritated. And then angry, accusing...

'It's your fault, Daniel...'

Mia was coming back now, holding the phone out, just as the stylist came over.

'Mia, we need to get you into the next swimsuit.'

Daniel took the phone and said, 'You're doing really well.'

She looked embarrassed. 'I'm so not prepared for this, and I'm not sure what you're looking for. I hope it's okay.'

Daniel took her by the hand and said over her head to the stylist, 'Two minutes, please?'

He led Mia over to the laptops where they were looking at the images, and the crew faded discreetly away to let Daniel show Mia what they'd done.

Eventually, she said, 'Wow, that doesn't even look like me.'

'It *is* you.' Her humility struck Daniel again. Her lack of ego.

She said, 'The jewellery isn't like anything you've done before. Is it a new line?'

Daniel nodded. 'It's a capsule collection, called Delphine. It'll test the market to see if there's an appetite for a more modern design along with the legacy and classic designs we do.'

'I like it. It feels fresh and new.'

Daniel watched as the stylist took Mia into a makeshift tent to change. *Fresh and new.* Like their relationship. Because after that incendiary kiss last night Daniel was even more determined to convince Mia that they could start afresh.

By day two of the shoot Mia was feeling a little more comfortable and confident—helped by the fact that the photographer was female, which was still not that usual on shoots like this. It reminded her that Daniel had always appreciated talent and skill over gender. A trait she'd found surprising in someone who came from a background steeped in history and legacy.

Day one had been a baptism of fire. It was a long time since she'd done a high-fashion, high-glamour shoot, and she'd got used to the world of catalogue modelling, which was all about trying to pack in as many different outfits in one day. Whereas this was much slower and more intense, but more creatively satisfying.

Now that she knew what to expect, though, it left more room for her to be aware of Daniel. Yesterday, she'd barely noticed him, she'd been so intent on not messing up. And when he'd driven her home last night she'd been so tired it had taken all her energy just to spend some time with Lexi before putting her down for the night and following her into bed.

But now all she could feel was his eyes on her, and her skin hummed with awareness even as she listened to the photographer's instructions, contorting her body into various shapes that felt anatomically ridiculous, but which she knew would look amazing in the photos.

When they broke for lunch, which was provided al fresco by a local catering company, the stylist gave

Mia a wrap to cover up and she went over to put some food on a plate. Daniel was talking to one of the crew members, and Mia took the opportunity to go and sit on a fallen branch that was near the shoreline. They were shooting in a lush area of forest a little further down the coast from where Daniel's house was.

Mia was enjoying the peace, but then the back of her neck prickled, reminding her that she was still finely attuned to Daniel's proximity in a way that was seriously irritating. He came and stood beside where she sat, hands in the pockets of a pair of board shorts. In a short-sleeved polo T-shirt, he still managed to ooze a certain kind of elegance while also looking sexy enough to make Mia's insides twist with need.

'You're doing an amazing job, Mia.'

Mia shrugged, feeling self-conscious. 'Adele makes it easy to be in front of the camera.'

Daniel shook his head. 'The two of you are creating something very special.'

'Well…thank you.'

She risked another glance at Daniel. His sunglasses were on his head and he was looking at her, his mouth quirking. 'Was that hard to say?' he asked.

She scowled. She'd never been good at accepting compliments. He knew too much about her. And she'd revealed even more since she'd seen him again.

'Lexi and Odile—'

'Are fine,' he said. 'I just called them. They're having ice-cream in town.'

Mia felt a pang, missing her baby. As if hearing her thoughts Daniel said, 'They can come to the set one of these days, if you like.'

'That'd be lovely, thank you. I haven't spent much time away from her before. She's getting so independent.' Mia shot him a warning look. *'Don't say like mother, like daughter.'*

But Daniel looked serious. 'You're a good mother, Mia.' He shook his head, looking away. 'My mother was *not* a good role model. She was cold and angry. All the time. Unhappy with my father, mainly. She viewed us children as irritations. Once she'd done her duty by giving birth, her job was over.'

Renewed guilt lanced Mia. She hadn't been fair to him. She opened her mouth to say something, but just then Adele's assistant said from behind them, 'Mia? We're ready to go again.'

She closed her mouth and stood up. Daniel took her plate out of her hands. The stylist and hair and make-up team were approaching, to make her ready for the camera again.

When Mia started posing, she tried her best to block out what Daniel had just told her and the emotions it had aroused. But that only made her focus on his physicality, and her awareness of him was even more heightened. He stood behind where the laptops were set up, arms folded, distracting Mia with the bunched muscles of his arms. Distracting her from the thought of his cold and uncaring mother.

Much to her embarrassment, she couldn't control her body's reaction when his eyes rested on her. It was as if a layer of skin had been stripped back, removing any armour she might have had. Her nipples peaked into hard points under the thin, stretchy material of the latest swimsuit she was wearing, and even though

Adele called out for numerous minute adjustments to Mia's poses, she couldn't help her mind going to extreme places.

She remembered the feel of Daniel's hands on her body, urgent, strong. His mouth moving over her skin, leaving a trail of fire before closing over the tip of her breast, sucking the peak deep into his mouth, making her bite her lip so hard she tasted blood...

'Mia?'

Feeling dazed, Mia blinked at Adele.

The woman said, 'One more change and then I think we've got it for today. You've been a trooper.'

Mia studiously avoided Daniel's eye as she got up and stretched her limbs, diving into the cover-up kaftan and wishing she could dive into the sea, to wash away this burning ache in the pit of her belly. And another ache nearer her heart.

Damn Daniel Devilliers.

CHAPTER EIGHT

'WHERE'S MIA?' DANIEL asked one of the assistants.

They were packing up the equipment ready for the next location and the last day of the shoot, which would take place after the weekend. They would have worked through, but Adele had to fly back to New York for a previously booked job, so everyone else would have two days off in paradise.

The young man was sheepish. 'Sorry, boss, I forgot to tell you. She's gone for a swim in the sea.'

Immediately Daniel's insides tensed. He grabbed a towel, making his way to the beach. There was no sign of Mia, and he looked to the sea, which appeared unbelievably rough to him. Big waves crashed along the shore, sending up sprays of sea water.

People meandered along the shoreline, dogs at their heels. Children frolicked in the evening heat. Sunset was spreading across the horizon, bathing everything in a pink and red hue.

This really was the simple life—the *pura vida* that Costa Rica was famous for—and it was why Daniel had bought his house here on a whim. Because it had appealed to the part of him that wanted to cultivate a freer, less constricted life than the one he had had growing up. It wasn't something he'd analysed in great depth, but it had definitely been his most spontaneous purchase.

But now he wasn't thinking about any of that. He scanned the sea, growing more and more tense. No sign of her.

Just when he was starting to feel panic he saw her, waist-deep in the water, wading out. For a moment his heart stopped. He thought she was naked. But then he realised she was wearing a skin-coloured swimsuit. One of those they'd photographed her in earlier. Evidently they'd let her use it for her swim.

She came out of the water, body glistening, bringing her long hair over one shoulder and squeezing it. She looked like a goddess. Aphrodite. More than one person almost stumbled as they passed by.

Daniel forced oxygen to his brain. She was okay.

She looked up at that moment, as if she could hear his thoughts, and he saw how she tensed. She started walking towards him and he could see that she was self-conscious. It amazed him how she could be so beautiful and not take advantage of it, like every other beautiful woman he knew. But her lack of arrogance added to her allure. It was what had captivated him from the moment he'd seen her in real life.

She came closer. 'Sorry, am I holding you up?'

Daniel handed over the towel even as he lamented the fact that she would cover her body up. She took it and wound it around herself, tying it under her arms.

'No, not at all.'

She made a motion with her head towards the water.

'You should have a swim—it's glorious.' Then she frowned. 'Actually, I've never seen you use the pool at the house…don't you like swimming?'

A solid weight lodged in Daniel's gut. He knew he could say something flippant, but some force was compelling him to admit, 'I know how to swim, but I don't. Ever.'

Mia stopped. Eyes widening. 'Why not?' And then she said, almost to herself, 'You were weird that day… when you came back and saw me with Lexi in the pool… You said something about putting up a protective rail. Did something happen to you?'

Daniel regretted whatever force had compelled him to tell Mia something he'd never told anyone else in his life. But it was too late now.

'I told you my sister died…'

'Yes.'

'She drowned in the pool at our chateau.'

The pool that had subsequently been filled in and covered over.

Mia put a hand to her mouth. 'Oh, Daniel… I'm so sorry. She was only six?'

He nodded. 'We'd been playing. I ran back into the chateau to get something, and while I was gone I heard her scream, and then a splash. It seemed to take me for ever to run back to the pool…and when I got there she was floating face-down in the deep end. She'd only just started learning how to swim. She had no armbands on. I jumped in. I knew how to swim but I was panicking, and it was so deep. I tried to push her, to turn her over, but she was heavy. And then I couldn't breathe…she was on top of me… I blacked out—'

'You obviously nearly drowned too.' Mia's horrified statement cut through the painful memory.

'I suppose I did. I never saw it like that.'

'Where were your parents?'

Daniel's mouth thinned. 'Probably fighting. The gardener was the one who pulled us out…it was too late for Delphine, though.'

'Delphine… The new jewellery collection is named after her?'

Daniel nodded. How could he explain that everything he did was infused with the loss of his sister? She was one of the reasons he'd accepted his inheritance— because she'd always loved the jewels so much. At every step along the way he was aware of how old she would be now. How beautiful. Living her life. And it was *his* fault. He hadn't been able to protect her.

Mia was shaking her head. 'You blame yourself, don't you?'

Yes. But he didn't admit that to Mia. 'My mother blamed me for Delphine's death. They were pretty much the last words she said to me before she left the chateau for good. For years I thought I was the reason she'd left… But then I found out that she'd been having an affair.'

Mia looked angry. 'She was projecting her own guilt onto you.'

'Perhaps. But the fact remains that I was there. I should've been watching Delphine. I *knew* we couldn't count on our parents for care because they'd never given it.'

Mia said, 'I trained as a lifeguard as a strong, athletic teenager, and I know how difficult it is to save someone panicking or unconscious in the water. It's almost impossible unless you're strong and trained. You were nine.'

When she put it like that, Daniel could appreciate it was perhaps irrational to blame himself, but Mia's words weren't any comfort. They just rubbed along all the jagged edges he'd held deep inside him for years.

'It's in the past,' he said.

'But it's not, is it? Because it's still affecting you. You don't swim as a result.'

'I don't need to swim.'

'You might… What if—God forbid—something happened to Lexi? If I wasn't around…'

Daniel's blood ran cold at the thought of history repeating itself. 'I would never put Lexi in danger. I'm going to arrange to get a protective fence around the pool.'

'You can put up all the fences you want, but accidents will still happen, Daniel. It was a tragic accident.'

Much later that night Daniel was in his study, staring into a glass of golden liquid. Golden liquid that couldn't burn away the seam of pain that had been exposed earlier. He still couldn't believe he'd told Mia about his sister and his mother. Even though he could see that she had a right to know.

Nevertheless, he resented the ease with which she seemed able to burrow under his skin before he knew it was happening.

He'd only come to his senses the first time around when he'd seen the hurt in Mia's eyes at the speculation in the paper about his possible engagement to Sophie

Valois. It had been like a bucket of cold water in his face, clearing the sensual haze in his mind.

But now that sensual haze was back.

Daniel cursed softly and tossed back the rest of his drink. If it was just about him and Mia, and the desire that had clearly not fizzled out, then Daniel would have no qualms about seducing her again and slaking his lust until whatever it was that bound him to her was well and truly burnt out. Then he could ignore those huge green eyes tempting him to spill his guts and get on with his life.

But it wasn't just about him and Mia. It was about Lexi too. And, like it or not, she called to every protective instinct he had.

He'd failed Delphine. But when he'd told Mia that today, instead of looking at him with horror, or judgement, she'd looked at him with pity. Compassion.

'It was a tragic accident.'

She didn't understand. She thought she could absolve him. But he knew nothing could. Except maybe a commitment to protect his daughter. And he would do whatever it took to—

Daniel's circling brooding thoughts came to a standstill when he heard a noise. He looked up and his pulse tripled, blood pumping in an instantaneous reaction to the sight before him.

Mia was standing in the open doorway, dressed in a T-shirt and, as far as he could see, nothing else. Her legs were endless and bare. Her hair was tangled and wild, tumbling around her shoulders. He could see the thrust of her breasts against the material of her shirt. Full and round. He'd spent the last couple of days in agony, looking at those perfect breasts, barely contained by the thinnest of swimsuits, each sexier than the last.

She looked as shocked as he felt. Eyes wide. Those same eyes that had looked at him earlier with such—

He blinked.

He told himself he was conjuring her up, like some form of mental torture. But, no, she was still there. Not a figment of his imagination. And now he saw that she was holding a water bottle in one hand and the baby monitor in the other.

He sat up. 'Mia?'

Mia swallowed. She shouldn't have come to explore why the light was spilling out of Daniel's office.

Unable to sleep, she'd gone to the kitchen to get some water and had seen the light.

Only to find Daniel staring into the bottom of a glass as if it held all the answers, long legs stretched out before him, in jeans and a T-shirt. Bare feet.

She hadn't been able to sleep because she'd been thinking of what he'd told her about his sister earlier…

Tension crackled in the air. 'I… I couldn't sleep… I didn't mean to disturb…'

Great—now she couldn't string a sentence together.

She started to turn around. 'Sorry, I'll—'

'Wait.'

She stopped, still facing away. But she could see Daniel reflected in the glass, behind her. He was standing. He'd put the glass down. She could see how his gaze dropped and moved over her legs, and suddenly it was hard to breathe.

'Don't go, Mia.'

Her heart was thumping so hard she felt light-headed. She watched as he came up behind her.

'Turn around.'

She knew that if she took a step, and then another, back towards her bedroom, Daniel would let her go. But the thought of *not* turning around was impossible.

She didn't know if it was the culmination of everything that had happened, or this magical place, or what he'd told her earlier, but she was no more capable of denying this pull any more than she was of stopping breathing.

She turned around.

Daniel was just inches away.

He took the water and the baby monitor out of her hands and put them down on a table.

At that moment Lexi gabbled something unintelligible, breaking the silence, and Mia froze.

Daniel asked, 'Is she awake?'

Mia waited a second and then shook her head. 'No. She talks in her sleep. It scared the life out of me the first time she did it. Now I sleep through it.'

An expression crossed Daniel's face. Something nakedly emotional. 'Delphine used to do that too.'

Mia's heart clenched. 'Daniel... I'm so—'

But he put a finger to her mouth. His eyes roved her face. His hand moved to the back of her neck, where it was hot and damp under the heavy fall of her hair.

'I want you, Mia.'

Right here, right now.

He didn't have to say it. She could feel it pulsing between them.

'I…' She hesitated for a moment. As if she had a choice. As if she could just walk away from this man and the fact that he was the one who had truly awoken her. As if she could walk away from the need that had been building ever since she'd seen him again. The need to sate the deepest craving she'd ever felt.

He was Lexi's father.

That knowledge sent something primal through her. Possessive. Her man.

'I want you too.' Her voice was rough with need, and she realised that she was giving herself permission to do this. Pushing aside the consequences.

He tugged her closer, until they were almost touching, and then he brought his other hand up, caught her chin, angled her face towards him and covered her mouth with his.

Mia combusted on contact. The kiss turned deep in seconds, tongues twining. Mia relished Daniel's taste, sucking him deep. She groaned. Or he groaned.

His hands moved down to her T-shirt, pulling it up. She lifted her arms. They broke the kiss and Daniel pulled the garment off. Mia's breasts felt heavy under his appreciative gaze, which devoured her. He'd always made her feel so…beautiful.

He cupped one breast and rubbed a thumb back and forth over one hard nipple. Mia bit her lip.

'Si belle…' So beautiful.

It was too much. Mia could feel emotion threatening to rise.

She said, 'You… I want to see you too.'

Daniel looked at her before taking his hand off her

and pulling his T-shirt off, behind his head and over. Now they were both bare from the waist up.

Mia sucked in a breath at the expanse of wide, muscled chest covered with dark hair. She put her hands on him, feeling the heat and the strength. Exploring the ridges of muscle and the flat discs of his nipples. Her nail caught on one and he sucked in a breath, took her hand.

He took her out to the deck outside the office, where there were two loungers. He said, 'Lie down.'

Mia did, before her legs could give out. She lay back and watched as Daniel's hands went to his jeans and snapped them open. Pulled down the zip. And then he yanked them down and off, kicking them aside. His underwear was despatched with equal efficiency, and Mia's eyes widened on that part of his anatomy—long, thick and hard. For her.

The fact that he hadn't slept with anyone else—and neither had she—was too much to absorb right now.

He came down on his knees and put his hands under her hips, tugging her down the lounger towards him. He pulled her underwear off and down her legs, throwing the wisp of material aside.

They were both naked, but Mia had never felt less self-conscious.

'Open your legs,' Daniel instructed.

Mia did, and heat washed up from her core when she saw how Daniel looked at her. He put his hands on her thighs and pushed them wider, and then he hooked her legs over his shoulders before coming down and placing his mouth…*right there*. At the centre of her body.

His hands were under her buttocks, holding her. She

had nowhere to hide as Daniel laid her bare and feasted on her sensitive flesh, exploring her with his tongue, stabbing deep, licking, sucking. It didn't take Mia long to tip over the edge, pleasure rocketing through her body before she could try and hold it back. It had been so long, and she'd never expected that it would be this good again…

Daniel lifted his head and she saw him smirk. She didn't even have the energy to make a face. Her blood was pumping too hard and her heart was beating too loudly.

'Still so responsive.'

Daniel came up on his knees between Mia's spreadeagled legs. He reached for something in his jeans pocket, and then she heard foil rip and watched as he pulled a protective sheath over his straining erection.

Good, she thought, even as she lamented the lack of skin-on-skin sensation. They didn't need to create any more drama. Just pleasure.

He surveyed her body, laid out before him, and it didn't even bother her. It sent fresh spirals of need through her, making her desperate.

'Please, Daniel…'

Answering her plea, he came down over her body and with one smooth, cataclysmic thrust seated himself deeply inside her. To her horror, she felt tears prick her eyes—not because of the earth-shattering sensation of Daniel's big body penetrating hers, but because of the emotion it evoked.

She lifted her hips, urging him silently to move, and with a muttered curse he did. Slowly. Pulling back out, almost all the way before thrusting back in again. Over and over again. Until the emotion was driven away by pure physical sensation and their bodies were covered with a fine sheen of perspiration.

Mia couldn't take her eyes off Daniel as he caught one of her legs and pulled it up, hooking it over his waist, deepening his penetration. Mia almost cried out but held it back, aware of the hushed night around them.

Daniel's movements grew less smooth, faster, harder, and Mia wrapped her other leg around his waist. The tension in her body was starting to tighten and spiral as the crescendo rose between them, all the way, inexorably, until Daniel said in a rough voice, 'Let go, Mia, fly.'

But in spite of her desperation something stubborn inside her made her shake her head. 'You first...'

Daniel's eyes went wide. She felt the tremor moving through his body as he fought for control, and then he uttered just one rough, indecipherable word as he thrust deep enough to touch her heart, and his whole body tensed as his climax ripped through it.

And that was the moment when Mia couldn't hold back any longer, with pleasure exploding at her core and crashing through her body in wave after endless wave, her intimate muscles contracting around Daniel's body until she was limp with exhaustion.

After long moments of their breath returning to normal, and with Daniel's body a heavy but delicious weight on hers, he lifted his head and said, 'You'll pay for that.'

Mia lifted a hand and touched Daniel's stubbled jaw. 'I was right behind you.'

She only noticed her hand was trembling when Daniel caught it and pressed a kiss to the middle of her palm. *Damn*. That emotion stirred again. Forcing him to lose control first hadn't made her feel any more in control herself.

Mia said, 'I should go…check Lexi…'

Daniel disengaged his body from hers and Mia winced when over-sensitive muscles protested. She couldn't quite believe what had just happened, even though she knew well that she'd been with him every step of the way.

She didn't want to think too closely about what it meant. But she was already very afraid that tasting Daniel again had sparked a renewed hunger that would be hard to satisfy.

She sat up with effort, just as Daniel reappeared with his jeans on, unbuttoned, holding out her T-shirt. She slipped it over her head, avoiding his eyes. He put out his hand and she looked up. His face was unreadable, and that comforted her somehow.

She put her hand in his and let him pull her up. He kept hold of her hand and led her back up to her bedroom suite. They stopped outside. She tried to take her hand back, but he held it until she looked at him.

'No regrets, Mia.'

She swallowed the regret already forming and pushed it back down. She'd chosen this.

She shook her head. 'No regrets.'

When Mia woke up she was disorientated, and her body felt achy but in a pleasant way. She shot up as soon as the events of last night came back to her in glorious Technicolor, a mixture of cold horror and heat rushing through her.

The sun was already high outside, and Lexi wasn't in her cot, which only compounded Mia's sense of disorientation. And then she heard it: the sound of Lexi's mostly unintelligible babble. Maybe Odile had come in and got her? Although Mia didn't think the young woman would feel that familiar yet...

Which left only one other possibility...one that Mia couldn't quite imagine.

She got up and washed her face, tried not to notice the faint stubble burn along her jaw. She threw on underwear and a pair of cut-off jeans, and a sleeveless shirt that tied at her waist.

When she arrived on the kitchen/dining level, nothing could have prepared her for the sight before her. Daniel was sitting at the table and Lexi was in a highchair. She wore a pretty floral romper suit and her hair was held back with a clip.

'Baba!' Lexi declared loudly, while banging a plastic spoon up and down on the table of the highchair.

Mia could see a spray of various foodstuffs in an almost perfect arc around the chair. They hadn't seen her yet as she was hidden by a wooden pillar.

Daniel shook his head. 'No, that's you.' He pointed to himself. *'Papa—c'est moi.'*

Lexi pursed her lips, as if she was trying very hard, and then said, 'Abba!'

Daniel shook his head again. *'Non, cherie,* that's a Swedish pop group. It's *Papa.'*

Mia felt a rush of conflicting emotions. Relief. Pride. Concern. Protectiveness. *Vulnerability.*

Still too raw after last night. She'd almost thought it might have been a lurid dream, but the aches in her body were too real—especially the ache between her legs. And she felt emotional to see the two dark heads so close together. Lexi was her father's daughter. Of that there could be no doubt.

Then Lexi spotted her. 'Mama!'

Daniel looked around. Mia's heart skipped a beat. She moved forward, trying to appear blasé. Nonchalant. As if what had happened last night and what was happening right now wasn't as earth-shattering or significant as it was.

'She'll say it when you're least expecting it. That's how she likes to roll. She takes her own time.'

Mia picked Lexi up out of the highchair, kissing her and making her giggle. She finally looked at Daniel and took in the fact that he was wearing jeans again, and a grey T-shirt that made his eyes look steely. She felt breathless when she recalled all too easily how he'd taken off his jeans with such efficiency last night…

'You should have woken me,' she said. She couldn't believe she'd slept through Daniel taking Lexi this morning.

He sat back. His jaw was clean-shaven. He looked as if he'd had twelve hours' uninterrupted sleep when she felt far too crumpled and raw.

'Actually, Odile heard Lexi chattering to herself. She asked me if she should go in and get her, so you could sleep, and I told her I'd do it.'

So Odile had noticed that Mia had been all but rendered unconscious by this man this morning. Brilliant.

'I will admit that Odile changed her nappy, so I can't claim that.'

Once again Mia felt it strange to acknowledge that she was no longer on her own with Lexi. 'That was sweet of her.'

'I told her she could take the day off because we'd be going out.'

'We are?'

Daniel nodded. 'If you like. There's a waterfall not too far from here. Gabriela is happy to make up a picnic.'

Mia felt unaccountably resistant to the idea, while at the same time knowing she was being ridiculous. If Daniel wanted to spend time with Lexi, that was a good thing. But after sleeping with him she felt as if the whole situation was morphing out of her control faster than she could try to control it.

At a total loss as to know what alternative she had, and feeling as if she was stepping off a ledge into very unknown territory, all she could do was nod and say, 'I'll change Lexi into something more suitable.'

'I insist,' Odile said. 'I've had the whole day off and I'd be more than happy to babysit Lexi. That's why I'm here, after all. And I'm going to put her cot in my room so you can get a decent night's sleep.'

Mia glared at Daniel above Odile's head. This was *his* sneaky doing. Arranging to take her out for dinner and conspiring with Odile. And she hated the betraying little frisson of anticipation that sizzled in her blood at the thought of going on a 'date'.

Where was her resolve from earlier?

Mia feared it had been fatally eroded due to spending the entire day with Daniel and watching him bond with his daughter. Not to mention the fact that she'd been in a weakened and susceptible state since last night.

She threw up her hands. 'Okay, fine. I'll get changed.'

She swore that if Daniel so much as smirked she'd change her mind, but he seemed to have the presence of mind not to push it.

She grumbled at herself as she took a quick shower and changed into a very plain sundress that she'd found in the dressing room. Dark green, thin straps. A little scallop detail around the edges, buttons down the front. Sandals.

She put her hair up in a rough bun and didn't bother with make-up. She didn't want Daniel to think she was making an effort, as if this was a real date. But her belly flip-flopped to think of exactly where they stood now. After last night. After today.

The day had passed far too easily and pleasantly in a national park. Lexi had loved the exotic colourful birds flying over their heads, and Daniel had carried her in a papoose against his chest, making Mia feel positively, shamefully, weak-kneed.

They'd conversed easily. It had reminded her painfully of how it had been between them before. How it had always taken her by surprise that she felt so comfortable with a man like him. It had reminded her of how close she'd come to hoping for more from Daniel.

But she'd excised those feelings from her heart. No matter how much he tugged on her emotions now she would not be so foolish again. She couldn't let him continue this seduction, because she knew that, no matter what their physical connection said, emotionally Daniel was not available.

He'd never wanted a baby, or a family, and he was only making this effort now because he felt a sense of responsibility.

By the time Mia and Daniel arrived at a charming two-level restaurant in the pretty little town of Santa Teresa she was almost rigid with the effort it was taking not to respond to Daniel—casually sexy in linen trousers and a white shirt that stretched almost indecently across his broad chest.

The same chest where he'd cradled their daughter for most of the day. An image that Mia could not get out of her head.

When he put his hand on her back to guide her into the restaurant she tensed even more, earning a frowning glance. But the maître d' approached before Daniel could say anything, fawning over them and taking them up to the top outdoor level and leading them over to a secluded table set out on a small balcony, overlooking the town and the sea beyond.

A full moon hung low in the lavender-hued sky. Candles flickered in the gentle breeze. It was simple and rustic and elegant all at once. There were small posies of local flowers in the middle of the table. Soft music played, and Mia recognised a world-famous Cuban band.

When the maître d' had left, Mia said, 'You really didn't have to go to this trouble.'

Daniel sat back. 'I like to eat, and we know you like to eat—it's no trouble.'

She would have scowled at him, but a waitress approached to give them water and tell them the specials.

When she was gone, Daniel sat forward. 'You look beautiful tonight.'

Mia looked at him suspiciously. Her dress really wasn't special. She'd made no great effort. She wondered if Daniel was making a point. She looked around and saw women in sleek tunic dresses, limbs glowing with their Costa Rican tan. Men in suits. Gold jewellery catching the light. Perfume scenting the air.

She felt churlish now. Guilty. 'I probably should have made more of an effort.'

Daniel shook his head, mouth quirking. 'You really don't know how beautiful you are.'

Now she blushed. 'You don't have to say that.'

'It's true. When the Delphine campaign is launched, your life is going to change. You'll be in serious demand.'

Mia rolled her eyes. 'I doubt that. I've never been in high demand and that's okay with me.' Before he could say anything else to seriously unsettle her, Mia said, 'This is all very nice, but you need to know that I'm not here to be seduced, Daniel. Last night was…a mistake.'

A mind-blowing mistake.

She shook her head. 'It can't happen again.'

The waitress came back with a bottle of white wine and poured it. Daniel lifted his glass and held it out. *'Salud.'*

It was as if she'd said nothing.

Mia clinked her glass on his and said, 'I mean it, Daniel.'

She'd braced herself for any number of things Daniel might say, so when he said, 'You're probably right,' she felt a shameful rush of disappointment. She hadn't expected him to agree with her.

He took a sip of wine and then looked at her. 'But if you think you're strong enough to resist what's between us then you're stronger than I am.'

Mia felt panicky. She should have known he wasn't giving in. 'But it's just…chemistry. It'll burn out.'

'It hasn't burnt out in two years.'

Mia's insides quivered. No, it hadn't. And Daniel hadn't slept with anyone else in two years. That reminder made all sorts of illicit emotions spiral inside Mia.

Their starters arrived and for once Mia was barely aware of the food—a deliciously light seafood chowder.

Somehow they managed to keep to neutral topics while eating, as if there wasn't a thick undercurrent of tension running between them, but when they'd finished eating he said, 'I only realised after you told me about your first boyfriend what a betrayal it must have been to learn of the agreement between me and Sophie Valois. No wonder it upset you.'

Mia's insides went into freefall. She hadn't expected Daniel to think of that. She shrugged minutely, as if that moment hadn't destroyed her as much as she hated to admit it had.

'It was coincidental,' she said.

'Still… I'm sorry.'

She looked at him, her precious defences wobbling. 'How were you to know?'

His mouth quirked. 'You did a very good job of not revealing anything much about yourself or your life.'

All designed to keep him out and keep herself safe. Which had not worked.

She felt defensive. 'You weren't exactly an open book either.'

'I met my match in you. I was used to women seeking to unearth as much personal detail as possible. You were…refreshingly uninterested. But then I found myself resenting your lack of interest slightly.'

They were interrupted by the waitress with coffee before Mia could fully absorb that and figure out what it might mean. She sipped the rich, dark drink, hoping that it would dispel some of the intensity she felt in these far too romantic surroundings.

When a local came over to greet Daniel, Mia welcomed the distraction, and the diversion from her urge to point out that, contrary to what Daniel had believed, she'd been far *too* interested in him. And that holding him at arm's length had been the hardest thing she'd ever done. And ultimately futile.

CHAPTER NINE

WHEN THEY ARRIVED back at the house a short time later, Mia felt ultra-aware of Daniel. In spite of her best intentions and instinct for self-preservation, she feared that today and then this evening had fatefully worn down her will to resist the temptation Daniel offered. It hummed between them…the invitation.

He turned around to face her. The house was silent. Mia felt a mixture of panic and illicit excitement.

Ridiculously nervous, she said, 'I should check on Lexi.'

'She's in Odile's room.'

'Oh, yes,' she said weakly.

Daniel wasn't fooled for a second. He moved closer and Mia refused to let him see how conflicted she felt. She knew she should walk away…but she couldn't. She felt bound to him in a way that she hadn't felt before.

He brought his hand up, trailing a knuckle lightly along her jaw, which was almost as incendiary as if he'd kissed her.

'Mia, you know I want you. But, like I said, if you're strong enough to resist this then I won't push you.'

Mia's heart thumped so loud she was sure it must be

audible. She swallowed. 'Last night…today… I don't know what's happening…where we are. How to…navigate this…'

'What's happening is inevitable when the chemistry is this strong. Maybe instead of fighting it, trust that it's taking us in the right direction. As a family. We're a family now, Mia, no matter what.'

It was that word that seemed to dissolve the last of the barriers that Mia had been so intent on throwing up. The chatter in her head stopped. She wanted Daniel. She'd never stopped wanting him. She'd used to look at men and wonder why they left her cold. Would any other man ever turn her on again?

The answer was standing right in front of her, and suddenly it seemed so simple.

'Trust that it's taking us in the right direction.'

All Mia knew right now was that there was only one direction she could go.

Towards the fire.

She stepped forward and reached up, wrapping her arms around Daniel's neck. Eyes fixed on his mouth. Firm and sensual. Anticipation mounted.

'Take me to bed, Daniel.'

He bent down slightly and suddenly Mia was being lifted into his arms. He carried her through the stunning house perched on a hill between the sea and the tropical forest and laid her down on his bed as if she was made of china.

He stripped himself bare and then, oh, so slowly, undid the buttons on her dress, one by one, kissing each piece of flesh as it was revealed, lavishing long moments on her breasts, until Mia was begging and writhing and panting.

Only then did he remove the rest of her clothes and, after donning protection, join his body to hers with such a powerful thrust that she was helpless against the spontaneous waves of pleasure that exploded from her core, wrenching any sense of control out of her grasp, making a mockery of her attempt to feel as if she'd been the one in control last night.

When Mia woke up, the first thing she noticed was the lingering sense of Daniel's arms around her, even though she knew she was alone in his bed. She stretched luxuriously, her limbs deliciously heavy and a sense of deep satisfaction flowing through her blood.

She couldn't even begin to analyse what had happened last night; she just knew that on some level she'd trusted Daniel enough to capitulate.

Trust. She'd thought she'd never trust anyone ever again after her first boyfriend. But she did trust Daniel. With Lexi, at least. His growing bond with her was genuine. Mia was sure of it.

As for herself, physically what they had was more than tangible. It was explosive. Last night had proved that. But emotionally… Mia knew she'd be very naive if she thought for a second that sharing confidences meant that things had changed.

She heard Lexi's babble and got up, not wanting to think too much about what Daniel had meant by moving forward as a family. She blushed when she picked up her dress and pulled it on, recalling Daniel undoing each button so slowly.

'Morning.'

She looked up from doing up enough buttons to be decent to go back to her room and take a shower. No underwear underneath. Daniel was wearing shorts and a T-shirt, no shoes, and he looked rested and…smug. Too smug for Mia's liking.

Her hair felt like a rat's nest, tumbled around her shoulders. She must look a sight. She'd been so weak…

As if reading her mind, he said, 'Don't be hard on yourself. I'm quite irresistible, you know.' He handed her a cup of coffee and Mia's heart lurched at this side of him she hadn't seen since they'd been lovers the first time. Flirtatious. Playful. Funny.

She took the coffee and resisted the urge to throw it over his head.

He said, 'I've told Odile to take the rest of the day off. Lexi has had breakfast and I'm going to take her down to the beach. Join us when you're ready.'

Once again, the ease with which Daniel was becoming a part of their lives was disorientating. Feeling prickly and exposed, Mia said, 'Make sure she's got sunscreen on, and a hat.'

Daniel's smugness increased. 'Of course. And Odile has packed a bag with essentials.'

He disappeared, and Mia stood staring stupidly at the empty space he'd left behind for a long moment before she finally moved.

A little later, feeling somewhat refreshed after a shower and some breakfast, and dressed in cut-off jeans and a T-shirt, Mia made her way down to the beach. She spotted Daniel and Lexi and walked towards them.

They were building a sandcastle and there were various items strewn around them. Toys, buckets, shovels.

Daniel looked up, shades covering his eyes. He should have looked ridiculous, cavorting with a toddler, but he didn't. Damn him.

Lexi stood up and came and grabbed Mia's hand. 'Mama, play.'

Mia dutifully let her daughter drag her down to the sand. Lexi handed her a bucket and said something incomprehensible.

Daniel said, 'I find it's best to pretend you know what she's saying.'

Mia's heart clenched at this further evidence of Daniel and Lexi bonding, even as every self-preserving instinct she had urged her to grab her daughter and run, far away. Which obviously was not an option.

Growing tired of bossing them around, Lexi wandered off a little way to fill her bucket with sand.

Daniel caught Mia's arm when she moved to follow. 'Wait a second. I want to say something.'

Mia looked at him warily. 'What?'

He pushed his shades onto his head. 'I know I mentioned marriage before—'

Mia stood up in one fluid motion, panic galvanising her movements. He was too close. Things were moving too fast for her to be able to assimilate how she felt. 'No way. I'm not talking about this again.'

Daniel stood up too. 'Just hear me out. You don't have to say anything now.'

Mia folded her arms, but she didn't walk away and she didn't say anything else.

'When I mentioned it before it was a reflex. I admit

that. I saw it as a solution to a problem. But now…
now I really mean it, Mia. I want us to marry and be
a family. Because we *are* a family, whether you like
to admit it or not. I don't want Lexi growing up on the
other side of the city, only to see her once a week or
less. I want her to be with me every day.'

A ridiculous dart of envy made Mia say tartly, 'And
me? Do I fit into this neat equation?'

Daniel took a step towards Mia and snaked a hand
around the back of her neck. His gaze roved over her
face and she saw the lick of heat in his eyes. An answering heat bloomed in her belly.

'Of course you do. I want you, Mia. You know that.
I haven't stopped wanting you, and the more I have
of you, the more I want. We have amazing chemistry. We like each other. We respect each other. And
we have Lexi.'

But I don't love you. That was what he omitted to
mention.

'You never wanted this, remember?' Mia couldn't
quite keep the bitterness out of her voice.

'I know. But that was before Lexi existed. I don't
regret Lexi, Mia—not for a second. Neither of us had
the family experience we wanted. She deserves more.'

Damn him. She'd told him too much.

They stared at each other for a long moment. And
then, from a few feet away, came, 'Papa!'

Mia saw the shock on Daniel's face. He dropped
his hand and looked at Lexi. 'What did you say, *mignonne*?'

He went over and bent down. She said, very clearly,
'Papa make castle.'

Papa. Mia put a hand to her mouth, emotion rising before she could stop it. Tears pricked her eyes. Daniel looked up at her and she couldn't hide the emotion.

He said, 'I'm just asking you to think about it, okay?'

Mia swallowed the lump in her throat. She owed him that much at least. She nodded.

That night Mia lay wide awake in bed, Lexi was on her back, legs and arms akimbo, in the cot nearby. She'd come to bed early, using Lexi as a pretext, afraid that Daniel would look at her and scramble her brain cells again—or, worse, touch her and make her agree to something she really wasn't sure she was ready for.

Marriage.

She'd always thought she was against the idea after her upbringing, until her first boyfriend had exposed her weakness for the dream. She'd learnt a harsh lesson. And then, with Daniel, she might not have dreamt of marriage, but she'd certainly come close to letting her defences down, to trusting him.

And she'd been humiliated again with the news of his arranged marriage. Reminded of her unpalatability. The fact that Daniel had acknowledged that last night only made her feel more vulnerable now.

And yet Mia knew that hundreds of thousands of marriages started with a lot less and lasted for a long time. Chemistry, respect…a child. Those were all solid foundations on which to build a lasting partnership. She'd convinced herself she would be happy with such a union, built on respect and mutual trust.

But she knew she wanted more. She wanted Daniel

to love her as she still loved him. It was pointless trying to keep denying how she felt. She'd fallen for him two years ago and she hadn't stopped loving him, no matter what she might have told herself. Now she was fathoms deep, with no hope of escape. And the fact that he was growing to love Lexi and building such a good relationship with her only made her love him more.

Mia turned over and thumped the pillow, trying to plump it up. What it really came down to was this: was she selfless enough to sacrifice her own happiness for her daughter's?

In her heart of hearts, she knew there was only one answer to that.

The following day was the last day of the ad campaign shoot. They were down at the edge of the sea this time. So far Daniel had kept his distance from Mia, which she'd been simultaneously grateful for and irritated by.

Odile had brought Lexi to visit the set today, and Daniel was behind the table of laptops, monitoring proceedings with Lexi in his arms.

Everyone had *oohed* and *aahed* over Lexi—who had, of course, lapped up the attention.

It was seriously distracting. But Mia focused as best she could and eventually the assistant called out, 'That's a wrap on Delphine, everyone! Great job!'

Mia felt wrung out, but also exhilarated, if she was honest. She'd never worked with this calibre of crew and it had been a whole new experience, demanding things of her she hadn't been sure she could deliver. But she had.

Adele came over and hugged her impulsively. 'You

were fantastic, Mia. Seriously, you need to prepare yourself for global attention once people see these pictures.'

Mia hugged her back. 'Well, I hope so, for your sake, but I really don't mind.'

Adele slid an expressive glance to where Daniel was handing Lexi back to Odile. She said with a wry smile, 'I guess I can't blame you. You have a beautiful family, Mia. I wish you all the luck in the world.'

Family. It would be up to her if they were actually to become a family.

Trying to block out the sense of impending pressure, Mia went with the stylist to the tent, to change out of the last outfit and back into her jeans and a shirt. She wiped off as much of the make-up as she could.

When she emerged nearly everyone was gone. She saw Odile walking back up the beach with Lexi, towards the house. Daniel was standing looking out to sea. A safe distance from the incoming tide. That detail made Mia's silly heart clench.

She knew this was it. He'd be expecting an answer.

She went and stood beside him, her body humming with awareness just to be near him.

He said, without looking at her, 'We'll fly to New York tomorrow for a couple of days, before returning to Paris.'

Mia barely heard him. Her answer was rising up inside her, and she was afraid if she didn't get it out she might change her mind.

'Okay,' she blurted out.

Daniel turned to look at her. 'Okay...to New York?'

Mia looked at him. 'No, I mean, yes…whatever. I mean, okay, I'll marry you.'

He went still. 'Are you sure?'

No!

But she nodded. 'Yes, it's the best thing…for Lexi.'

'What about you?'

'Like you said, we have chemistry, respect…'

'Is that enough for you?'

No.

Mia searched Daniel's expression to see if she could see even a smidgeon of something…but he just looked genuinely concerned. Which was even worse.

Without answering him directly, she said, 'You're right. I want more for Lexi too, and she deserves two loving parents, together.'

But just not in love with each other, hissed a little voice.

She pushed down her misgivings.

Daniel closed the distance between them and cupped her face in his hands, tipping it up to his. He smiled, and for a moment Mia could almost pretend that maybe—

'You won't regret this, Mia. I'll do my best to make you and Lexi happy. I promise.'

He covered her mouth with his and Mia stretched up, wrapping her arms around his neck, bringing her body as close to his as possible. The familiar fire raced along her veins, heating her blood. She could feel his body responding to hers and she felt that if she could just have this effect on him…and if he could just never stop kissing her, making love to her…then maybe she could pretend that it would be enough to sustain her.

* * *

'You want us to get married in New York?'

Mia's voice was a hissed whisper across the aisle of the private plane that was taking them from San José to New York.

Daniel didn't like the look of sheer panic mixed with horror on her face. He shrugged. 'Why not?'

Her mouth opened and closed a few times.

She looked…amazing. She was wearing a light green silk shirt dress. Casual but sexy. Her skin was even more golden after their time in Costa Rica, and more freckles were liberally dotted across her nose. Her hair, too, had turned lighter, and she'd plaited it today. It hung over one shoulder, enticing Daniel to wrap his hand around it and pull her over to him so he could take that look off her face by kissing her.

He needed her.

She'd been packing last night, and by the time he'd wrapped up his own work she'd been in bed, with Lexi asleep too. He dragged his gaze back to her face. She was still looking stunned.

Finally she said, 'I thought we might have a period of engagement. To get used to the idea.'

Something curdled in Daniel's gut at that suggestion. The need to make Mia his wife ASAP was a compulsion he didn't want to analyse too deeply.

He reached across and took her hand. 'I want us to be a family, Mia. Why wait?'

Her eyes were huge. She bit her lip. 'Can it even happen that quickly?'

Daniel nodded. 'Once we obtain a licence, we can marry in twenty-four hours.'

She glanced behind, to where Odile was occupying Lexi with a game, the little girl chattering happily. Daniel saw Mia's expression soften and felt a spike of jealousy—at his own daughter! But then Mia looked back, and Daniel knew he didn't want that softness to go out of her expression.

He said, 'I want everyone to know you're my wife and that we're a family.'

Mia looked a little pale. 'I guess there's no reason why we should wait. Things aren't going to change, are they?'

There was a quality to her voice he couldn't quite decipher, but the rush of triumph drowned out the need to analyse it.

He took her hand and pressed a kiss to the palm, her scent filling his nostrils and heating his blood. 'I'll let my office know to obtain the licence.'

At that moment Lexi's voice rang out. 'Mama!'

Mia took her hand from his and made her way to their daughter.

It was the strangest sensation, but even though Mia had just agreed to marry him within the next few days, and Daniel had exactly what he wanted, he felt inexplicably as if something was slipping out of his grasp.

Later that afternoon, after they'd arrived at JFK and then taken a helicopter ride into Manhattan, during which Lexi had stayed wide-eyed and silent, they'd landed on a tall building which turned out to be owned by Daniel. It housed the North American offices of Devilliers, plus his private apartment and a shop on the ground level.

They were greeted by staff and taken down to the apartment—a vast, elegant, luxurious space with a terrace overlooking Fifth Avenue and the greenery of Central Park visible just a few blocks away.

Mia was looking around the fully stocked nursery which was across the hall from the master bedroom suite. She felt Daniel's presence behind her, and all the little hairs on her body stood up.

She didn't turn around, afraid he'd see something of the emotion she'd been feeling since earlier, when he'd told her he wanted to marry her as soon as possible.

'You really didn't have to kit out an entire closet full of clothes,' she said. 'She'll have outgrown most of them within a couple of weeks, she's growing so fast.'

'I'll ensure anything that isn't used is donated to charity.'

'That'd be good.'

'Mia.'

She turned around, careful to shield her expression. She felt too raw at that moment, as the enormity of their impending nuptials sank in.

Daniel was leaning against the doorframe, impossibly tall and broad. He said, 'My staff have obtained the marriage licence, and someone will come up with the paperwork you need to fill out shortly. They'll also have a pre-nuptial agreement for you to look at. All going well, we'll be getting married tomorrow afternoon.'

So it really was happening.

Mia's heart-rate sped up. This time tomorrow she would be Mrs Devilliers. Lexi would have two parents who loved her. She would be part of a family.

In spite of everything, Mia felt a tiny flame of hope flicker to life. Maybe by *becoming* a family they could truly be one. Daniel could grow to love her.

And then Daniel said, 'But first I need to give you something.'

Mia frowned. 'Wha...?'

Her voice faded when she saw Daniel take a box out of his pocket—a small velvet box—and she tensed. He opened the box and she sucked in a breath. It was a circular cut emerald ring, with two small diamonds on either side, in a platinum setting. It was simple and...perfect.

Daniel said carefully, 'This isn't like what happened to you before, Mia. This is the real deal. I would be proud and honoured for you to become my wife.'

She hated the emotion that clutched at her chest.

As if he'd been waiting for her tacit permission, he took the ring out of the box and picked up Mia's hand, sliding the ring onto her finger. It fitted.

Mia *knew* this marriage was really little more than a marriage of convenience, and yet right now it was hard not to hope that perhaps it could become something else.

She looked up at Daniel, but his expression was unreadable. Very quickly she doused the rogue emotions. She was losing it. She had to keep it together.

'Is it okay?' he asked.

Mia pulled her hand back. 'Yes, it's lovely.'

'You won't mind wearing it?'

Mia felt exposed again. 'I'm sure I'll get used to it.'

Daniel took a step back. He became brisk. 'I've arranged for a stylist and a hair and make-up team to come to the apartment. The stylist will bring a range of choices for you to choose a wedding outfit from. They'll also have clothes for Odile, who will be our witness, and Lexi. I have to go down to the offices, and I'll probably be working late, so you guys go ahead and eat dinner.'

Mia's head was spinning with all the information by the time he walked away. She found Odile feeding Lexi a late lunch in the kitchen. The young woman was beaming.

'I can't believe you're getting married tomorrow,' she said. 'It's so romantic.'

Mia smiled weakly. It couldn't be less romantic. 'You don't mind being a witness?'

Odile's eyes looked suspiciously shiny. 'I'd be honoured. You and Daniel and Lexi…you guys are amazing, and I've already seen so much of the world because of you.'

Mia gave her a quick, impulsive hug. She'd become very fond of the girl, and was glad of a grounding force when everything suddenly seemed to be spinning out of her control.

Within hours the apartment had become a hive of activity, with assistants from Daniel's office bringing paperwork to sign, and then the stylist and her team coming to help Mia prepare for the following day.

Mia signed the pre-nuptial agreement, which to her eyes would be ridiculously generous if she should ever divorce Daniel. The outlined custody arrangements in case of a divorce were also fair, and skewed in Mia's favour. She really had nothing to complain about.

By the time she and Odile and Lexi had eaten that

evening she was wrung out, and more than happy to crawl into bed not long after Lexi had gone down to sleep.

It was only when she woke a few hours later, instantly aware that Daniel was in the bed beside her, that she realised that of course the master suite was his room too. And, as his fiancée, of course she'd be sharing his room.

She didn't open her eyes and she held her breath, even so her body came alive, knowing Daniel was just inches away. But, as much as she was tempted to drown out all her concerns and doubts and fears by losing herself in the physical, she felt it was important in that moment to hold back. As if by not giving in to Daniel's silent but potent pull, she could exert some last vestige of control.

Somehow—miraculously—she managed to fall asleep, and she didn't wake when Daniel curled his body around hers and wrapped an arm around her waist, holding her to him.

When Mia woke the next morning she almost wondered if she'd dreamt that Daniel had been in the bed beside her last night. There was no sign of him now.

She heard Lexi babbling in her room and got up to tend to her, seeing a note on the pillow beside hers.

She picked it up.

Morning. I didn't want to wake you.

Mia's heart thumped. So she hadn't imagined him beside her.

The note went on.

I have to do some work at the office, but I'll be back at one p.m. to take you to the venue for the wedding.
D

Mia sighed. Not even an X. Her flicker of hope yesterday mocked her.

She got up and went to Lexi, her heart swelling at the sight of her beautiful baby girl. Picking her up and hugging her close, she told herself she was doing the right thing. Lexi would grow up secure and loved. By two parents. She would make this work.

A few hours later, Mia surveyed herself critically in the mirror. She'd chosen a very simple white Stella McCartney wide-legged trouser-suit, with a sheer lace body underneath. She'd matched it with white high heels, the pointy toes just peeping out from under the trousers. The only jewellery she wore was her engagement ring.

Her hair had been washed and blow-dried into big loose waves. Her make-up was minimal. She wanted to feel like herself as much as possible, and at all costs avoid anything floaty and romantic. This wedding was not about romance.

A hush went around the dressing room, where she'd been getting ready, and she looked up to see Daniel standing in the doorway in a steel grey three-piece suit. Jaw cleanshaven. He looked breathtakingly handsome.

And in his arms was Lexi, who was wearing a white dress, with a flower clip in her hair.

She put out her arms towards Mia. 'Mama…'

Mia could see that she was feeling a little overwhelmed with all the activity and cuddled her close. Lexi put her finger in her mouth.

Everyone who had been getting her ready melted away discreetly.

Daniel said, 'You look…stunning, Mia.'

She felt shy. 'Thank you, so do you.'

Odile appeared behind Daniel. She looked very pretty in a deep red maxi dress, her hair up. 'The car is downstairs when you're ready to go.'

Mia's heart pumped.

Daniel led the way to the elevator and down. The lobby of the building was empty except for some security men and the concierge, who said, 'Best wishes, Mr Devilliers and Miss Forde!'

Mia smiled. Lexi waved, perking up again.

Then they were in the car and heading to a hotel, where a room had been booked for them to have a private ceremony.

Once inside the beautiful Art Deco hotel—one of Manhattan's most exclusive—they were whisked up to a private suite by the manager. Apart from Odile there was a staff member from Daniel's office, acting as the other witness, and a handful of guests, some of whom she recognised as his legal team.

The ceremonial part of it was a bit of a blur to Mia, who still couldn't quite believe that it was happening. Daniel slid a plain gold band on the finger where her engagement ring had been—she'd put it on her other hand for the ceremony—and Odile handed her a slightly thicker ring for him, which she slid onto his finger, feeling something very possessive wash over her. Primal.

When Daniel kissed her at the invitation of the officiant Mia found herself tensing, aware of everyone watching them. She felt like a fraud and pulled back. Daniel frowned slightly, but then just took her hand and led her out of the room to the sound of everyone clapping.

'Do you mind that we didn't have a bigger reception?'

Mia looked at Daniel where he stood on the apartment terrace beside her. They were both holding champagne glasses. They'd returned a short while before and the staff had met them with a little fanfare and champagne. It had seemed churlish to refuse.

Daniel had taken off his jacket and his tie was gone, top shirt button open. She'd taken off her jacket too. And her shoes. Odile had just taken a very overtired Lexi off for a bath and then bed.

Mia shook her head. 'No, it was perfect. It's not as if it was a real wedding.'

'It *was* a real wedding. You're officially Mrs Devilliers now.'

A flutter came from deep inside Mia's belly. She stamped it out. 'You know what I mean. Anyway,' she said, 'I'm not really one for big glittering functions.'

Daniel leaned on the terrace wall and surveyed her. 'I hate to break it to you, but there'll be a few for you to go to as my wife.'

Mia immediately felt daunted, but forced a smile. 'I'm sure I'll cope.'

'I have no doubt you will. You're formidable, Mia.'

She shook her head, hating how his words made her feel, made that hope flicker. 'I'm really not—and you don't have to say those things. It's not as if you need to woo me, Daniel. We're married now.'

An expression crossed his face, but it was too fast for her to decipher. He said, 'Yes, we are married.'

Daniel moved closer and took Mia's champagne glass out of her hand, putting it down with his on a nearby table. He drew Mia into his arms and the thin material of her lace body and the silk trousers was no barrier to the heat and steely strength of Daniel's body, not to mention his arousal.

Instant heat flooded Mia, and unlike the previous night, when she'd felt the need to keep a bit of herself back, right now she desperately craved the exquisite oblivion Daniel could offer her. She needed to be reminded of what was binding them together apart from Lexi.

She stretched up, winding her arms around Daniel's neck. When he lowered his head, though, to cover her mouth with his, she moved instinctively, pressing a kiss to his hard jaw, avoiding that intimacy without really understanding why, knowing only that it was necessary in that moment.

'Take me to bed, Daniel.'

'Your wish, Mrs Devilliers, is my command.'

CHAPTER TEN

WHEN MIA WOKE in the morning she could hear the faint hum of Manhattan traffic far below. She'd always loved New York—it had been the first place she'd come to start her modelling career and she'd never forget that first view of Manhattan, coming across the bridge from the airport.

And now here she was, in one of those tall buildings. Married. A mother.

She lifted her hand and looked at the rings, nestled side by side. She hated to admit it, but she liked them. Liked the feeling that they marked her as Daniel's wife.

She sat up in bed, holding a sheet up to her chest, and winced when she saw the torn lace of the body she'd worn under her wedding suit. Unable to find the opening, Daniel had ripped it, making Mia gasp, but then he'd put his mouth to the heated flesh between her legs, hands cupping her buttocks, making her squirm and writhe under his wicked mouth, torn clothes forgotten.

There had been something almost desperate between them…insatiable…as Daniel had taken her over and over again. They had only fallen asleep as the dawn had risen outside.

The apartment felt silent and empty. Mia got up and had a quick shower, and dressed in a pair of casual trousers and a matching long-sleeved rust-coloured top, pulling her hair back into a loose ponytail.

The housekeeper, a genial older man, was in the kitchen. 'Good afternoon, Mrs Devilliers.'

Mia gasped and checked the time. It was after midday. She blushed profusely. 'I'm so sorry. I had no idea it was so late.'

'Don't be silly—you just got married. Can I fix you some brunch?'

'Um…where is everyone?'

'Odile has taken Lexi to the park, I believe, and Mr Devilliers is down in his office. He said you weren't to be disturbed.'

It was a long time since anyone had cared for her welfare. It was a strange feeling. Seductive.

'I'd love something small—maybe just an egg and toast? If that's not too much trouble?'

The housekeeper gave Mia a slightly funny look, before smiling and saying, 'That's no problem at all. And, please, call me Tom.'

'Thank you, Tom.'

After she'd eaten an exquisite brunch of scrambled eggs and smoked salmon, on delicate pieces of toast, Mia debated calling Odile and catching up with them, or going down to see Daniel.

She found herself acting on impulse, taking the elevator down to the main offices. She would find Odile and Lexi afterwards.

At the main reception area everyone was very friendly, and they showed her to where Daniel's corner office was. An older lady in the anteroom stood up and introduced herself as Martha. She said, *sotto voce*, 'He's on a call but I'm sure he'll be pleased to see you if you want to go in and wait. Congratulations on your marriage, by the way.'

'Thank you.'

Mia pushed at the heavy door, which was ajar, and went in, thick carpet muffling her footsteps. The first thing she noticed was the astounding views of Manhattan on both sides.

Daniel had his back to her. He was standing at the window and had his phone up to his ear and his other hand in his pocket. His back was broad under a white shirt, and her eye travelled down to those slim hips and taut buttocks.

And then he spoke, his voice low but distinct in the silence. 'Yes, we're married. It's the perfect solution. It takes the heat out of any potential news story and it'll defuse any interest in my daughter. We're a family unit now.'

The person on the other end was obviously speaking, and as what Daniel had said sank in, and Mia interpreted the businesslike tone of his voice, a cold chill crept through her.

Daniel sounded exasperated. 'Look, Nikki, it's done. She's the mother of my child, and if we hadn't married I couldn't have guaranteed that this wouldn't have ended up in the courts. She's no pushover and money doesn't sway her. This *is* the best solution to a potential PR nightmare. Returning to France unwed, with a child in tow, would have left us wide open to scrutiny and completely overshadowed the launch of Delphine, which is going to be challenging as it is—'

He suddenly stopped talking and turned around.

Mia wasn't sure why she was feeling so winded all of a sudden. Daniel hadn't said one thing she didn't already know. But to hear him lay it out like that, so cold and stark, had sliced right into her heart.

Daniel terminated the call and looked at her. 'Mia—'

She cut him off. 'That's why you brought us to Costa Rica, isn't it? Because you wanted to use that time to seduce me again and persuade me to go along with your plans.'

Daniel was nothing if not honest. 'Getting you away from the press *was* a concern. But I knew that I wanted us to be a family, yes. And I knew I wanted you. As for the marriage... I hoped that you'd agree. Because I do feel that this is the best outcome for all of us.'

She'd fallen into his plans within the week, like a ripe peach. She realised that even up to this moment she'd been harbouring a tiny illicit flame of hope for *more*. But what she'd just heard had killed that flame for good.

She forced breath into her lungs, dazed—and annoyed with herself for feeling blindsided. She couldn't even say that Daniel had manipulated her. She'd wanted him too. And she had agreed to the marriage of her own volition, for all the right reasons.

'Mia—'

She put up a hand, not wanting him to hammer home the message. It was loud and clear. Her emerald ring sparkled in her peripheral vision, mocking her. This one might be real, but it meant no more than the cubic zirconia necklace had.

'It's fine. I'm sorry I disturbed you. I just… I was actually on my way out to catch up with Odile and Lexi. They've gone for a walk.'

'I know. Security are with them.'

Mia turned around, but Daniel said, 'Wait.'

She turned around reluctantly. She just wanted to go—get away from that far too incisive grey gaze.

'Are you sure you're okay?'

She pinned a smile on her face. 'Absolutely fine. Will we see you later for dinner?'

'Actually, we're going to take an overnight flight back to Paris tonight, so you should probably prepare for that.'

'We'll be ready.'

Mia left the office and avoided catching anyone's eye. It was only when she was out on the street that she let her mask fall and put sunglasses over her eyes to hide the sting of tears, hating herself for the weakness.

Paris was grey under leaden skies when they returned from New York early the following morning. Odile had gone home, and Mia and Lexi were in bed, sleeping off the flight. Daniel was restless, and had come down to his office above the *salon*. But he was alone. It was too early for any staff to have arrived yet.

He wasn't remotely superstitious, but the slate-dark skies felt like some kind of omen and he scowled at himself.

He didn't like how the image of Mia standing in his

Manhattan office the previous morning kept coming back into his head. Her face had been pale, with the same stricken expression he'd only seen twice before. When she'd seen the leak in the newspaper about his proposed engagement to Sophie Valois, and when she'd come to tell him she was pregnant.

He recalled the conversation she'd overheard, his conscience pricking again.

He'd felt under pressure. His chief PR advisor had been freaking out at the news that Daniel and Mia were married, without any prior warning. Daniel had felt exposed. He knew marrying Mia in haste had been an impulse to make her his as soon as possible, out of a primal need that didn't have much to do with logic. And it was as if his PR advisor had intuited that.

But he'd reassured himself that everything he'd said to Nikki had made total sense. And it was every-thing Mia had agreed to. To make a marriage based on respect and mutual chemistry for the sake of their daughter.

Marrying Mia and ensuring Lexi's security and fu-ture was the right thing to do. He couldn't offer Mia empty platitudes and promises, much as he knew it might make things more palatable for her. But they were his family now, and he was going to do every-thing in his power to ensure that the toxicity of his past did not infect the future. He would do things differ-ently from his parents, and already he and Mia had a foundation stronger than anything he'd ever seen be-tween them.

It was enough. It would have to be.

So why was he feeling guilty?

That sensation of something precious slipping out of his grasp was haunting him again, mocking him. He pushed it down deep and told himself he was being ridiculous.

'I feel like you're avoiding me.'

Mia looked at Daniel across the dinner table at the end of the first week since they'd returned to Paris. 'What gives you that impression?'

Daniel arched a brow. 'The fact that this is the first meal we've shared since we got back to Paris, and the fact that you're not sleeping in my bed.'

A pang of sexual need gripped Mia. In spite of the deep vulnerability she felt around Daniel now, she couldn't dent the aching need at her core. Every night she had lurid X-rated dreams and woke up aching and frustrated in the morning.

'Lexi has been unsettled at night since we returned. I don't want to disturb you.'

'Where is Odile? I offered her a full-time job.'

'I told her she didn't need to start straight away.'

'The launch of the Delphine line of jewellery is next week. We'll have press junkets and the launch party to attend.'

An assistant of Daniel's had informed her of the schedule, and it alternately terrified her and excited her.

She looked at Daniel now. 'I've never been involved with anything this high-profile before.'

'I'll be right by your side.'

That thought should have comforted Mia, and it would have at any other time. But every minute she spent in close proximity to Daniel now left her terrified that she'd reveal her feelings, or he'd see something. And if he knew how she felt she wouldn't be able to continue pretending she was okay with a marriage in name only.

That was why she'd been avoiding him. Because she didn't know if she could truly do this. And she felt like a failure because she should be stronger for her daughter's sake.

People lived through marriages of convenience all the time—what was so special about her that she thought she deserved more? But Mia knew that she did. And so did Lexi. Living with Daniel and knowing that his feelings only ran to *like* and *respect* would wear away at her soul until she was a husk.

And that couldn't be good for Lexi.

Hearing Daniel during that phone call had brought home just how clinical he was about this marriage. And yet when he touched her he made her think that there was a chance of *more*.

But that was just sex.

That was why she couldn't let him touch her again.

And yet even as she thought that her body ached. The thought of not making love to Daniel ever again... That was obviously not something he would tolerate. Did she really want to drive him into the arms of a lover? The mere notion of that made Mia feel violent.

Daniel's gaze was narrowed on her face. 'Want to share your thoughts? You look like you want to commit murder.'

Desperation mounted inside Mia. Something had to give or she'd lose it completely. Clearly avoiding

Daniel and depriving them both of release was not
working, and it would only invite scrutiny and, yes,
possibly murder.

Could she do this and hide her feelings, not confuse
passion for emotion? She had to. Or she might as well
get up and leave now.

Baldly, before she lost her nerve or changed her
mind, she said, 'I want you.'

His eyes flared at that. 'Right here? Now?'

She blushed. She felt gauche, like the first time
she'd gone out with him. But he took pity on her, standing up and taking her hand, pulling her up from the
chair and leading her out of the dining room and down
to the bedrooms.

After Mia had checked on Lexi quickly, just across
the hall, she stepped into Daniel's bedroom. His shirt
was already off and the top button of his trousers was
undone. He closed the door behind her and caged her
in with his arms, hands either side of her head.

'Now, where do we start to make up for lost time?
This week has felt like a month, Mia.'

She reached up, pressing kisses to his jaw, her hands
exploring his chest, revelling in the feel of taut muscle
under hot silky skin. She pressed kisses there, trailing her mouth down, her hand finding the zip of his
trousers and pulling at it, then urging his trousers off
his hips along with his underwear, until they fell to
the floor.

He stepped out of them, kicked them aside. Still
wearing all her own clothes—a pair of trousers and a
silk top—Mia dropped to her knees and heard Daniel
suck in a breath. *This* she could handle, she thought, as

she wrapped her hand around Daniel's erection, which was straining towards her.

She took him into her mouth and his hands went into her hair. 'Mia…you don't have to…' But then his breath hissed out. *'Dieu, tu me tué.' You're killing me.*

Mia was ruthless, wringing every ounce of pleasure out of Daniel, and when she was done he lifted her up and stripped her bare, eyes feverish with pleasure and fresh desire. Like this, there was no time or room for words or tenderness. And that was how Mia would get through this and stay sane.

A few days later Daniel woke at dawn, as he habitually did, his body naked and feeling so heavily pleasured that he wasn't sure if he would be able to move. Every night he and Mia made love and fell asleep in an exhausted tangle of limbs. But when he woke she was gone.

Sometimes, like this morning, when the rush of last night's images came back into his head, he wondered if he was losing it. If he was hallucinating these torrid nights with his wife, when she disappeared like a ghost before dawn.

He couldn't put his finger on it, but something had changed. Making love to Mia had always been an incendiary thing, from the very first time, and it had only got hotter. But since they'd returned to Paris, there was an edge that Daniel hadn't noticed before.

It was as if she was deliberately doing her best to send him into orbit, with a pleasure so intense and all-consuming that his days were populated by fevered daydreams. As soon as he returned to the apartment they didn't even bother with the niceties of sharing dinner before tearing their clothes off. Dinner had become a midnight kitchen interlude.

Daniel cursed his introspection. Was he seriously analysing and scrutinising the fact that sex with his new wife was off-the-charts hot?

He got up and had a shower, before he lost it completely.

When he was on his way out of the apartment to go to work that morning, he paused at Lexi's bedroom door. It was open a crack and he pushed it open all the way. Lexi was on her back in the cot. Mia was in the bed on the other side of the room, also on her back, asleep, hair spread around her head in a wild tangle.

The bed that was for the nanny. Not his wife.

Immediately Daniel wanted to scoop her up and place her back into *their* bed. And then he wanted to bend down, wrap her hair around his hand, wake her with a deep, drugging kiss and have her beg and moan for mercy, in punishment for leaving him feeling weak after so much pleasure.

A little stunned at the intensity of his thoughts, Daniel stepped back. Mia moved minutely on the bed and he noticed slight shadows under her eyes. A faint tension around her mouth. Something wasn't quite right, but he couldn't put his finger on it. And Daniel instinctively shied away from looking too closely, telling himself again that he was being paranoid. They were in the honeymoon phase that every couple went through, and their marriage wasn't about regular intimacies like waking up together.

Everything was fine. What more did he want?

* * *

'So, Mia, can you tell us how you met Daniel Devilliers?'

Mia was totally out of her comfort zone, talking to the radio host, but she was doing her best to sound confident.

This was the last PR interview before the launch party for the new jewellery line this evening. She'd already seen the huge billboards featuring eye-catching images from the Costa Rica campaign, but the images were so hyper-stylised they didn't even really look like her.

Instead of marvelling over them, all she could think of was of the time she'd spent there with Daniel. Watching him bond with Lexi. Making love again for the first time. Discovering his fear of water, what he'd told her of his sister. All those moments that had felt tender, but which she knew now had been contrived to get her where he wanted her.

In his bed and shackled to his side.

'When did you know you were in love with your husband?'

Mia blinked and came back to the present moment. Maybe she'd misheard? 'I'm sorry, can you repeat the question?'

'Of course. We would love to know when you fell in love with your husband?'

Mia longed to say something blasé, but the memories of Costa Rica were still vivid in her mind's eye. She knew Daniel was outside the small radio studio, listening, and the words that she was terrified of speaking now tumbled out of her mouth, as if she knew she had a licence to say them without fear of censure.

After all, it was what everyone expected. They didn't want to hear that there was no love in their marriage. They wanted the fairy tale.

The problem was, so did she—in spite of everything.

She said, 'I think I always loved him…from the first moment I saw him. But we went our separate ways, and it wasn't until we met again that I knew I'd never stopped loving him. And then, when I saw him with Lexi, our daughter…that's when I knew I would love him for ever.'

The radio presenter sighed theatrically. *'Ah, l'amour…c'est fantastique, non?'*

They wrapped up the interview after that and Mia emerged, feeling a little dazed. Daniel led her to his car, and when they were in the back, speeding away, he tugged at his tie.

'You did well,' he said, and then, 'What is it with this obsession with romance and love? Everyone wants there to be some fairy tale story.'

He looked at her, and her skin prickled with awareness.

He said, 'You answered well. I almost believed you myself.'

Daniel's careless remark broke the last remaining barrier around Mia's heart. She'd spent the week trying to pretend that she could endure a purely physical relationship if she felt as if she was in control. But any sense of control was rapidly fraying at the edges. Maybe if he hadn't said the words *fairy tale* with such derision she wouldn't feel so reckless right now.

She wanted to dent that arrogant cynicism.

She turned to Daniel, an unstoppable force rising inside her. 'Actually, I answered it well because I wasn't making it up.'

Daniel's hand stilled on his loose tie. He looked at her. 'What?'

'You heard me.'

Mia's heart was thumping. Daniel said something to the driver, who put up the privacy partition, cocooning them in the back.

Then he shook his head. 'You're going to have to say that again.'

'What I said to that interviewer... I meant it. I didn't have to lie or make it up. I love you, Daniel. And, believe me, I wish I didn't. Because things would be so much easier. But I do. And I have done ever since we met. Even though I thought I hated you for a while... after the baby... I didn't really.'

Daniel looked shocked—stricken. 'But you agreed to this marriage on the basis of mutual desire...respect...you knew I wasn't offering more.'

Mia suddenly felt deflated. 'I know... And I thought I could do it, for Lexi's sake. But when we got married I couldn't help hoping that perhaps things might change. I was wrong.'

Daniel was shaking his head. 'My background broke me, Mia. I can't promise you—'

'More. Yes, I know.' Mia cut him off, not wanting to hear him spell it out.

She knew she'd crossed a line now, in articulating her feelings. But she couldn't continue to be physically intimate and yet have no emotional connection. Daniel believed he was broken. She couldn't fix him if he wasn't willing to be fixed.

She shook her head. 'I can't do this, Daniel. I'm sorry. I thought I could, but it'll destroy me to continue a charade…and I don't think that's good for Lexi either. You know what it was like to have unhappy parents. I won't do that to her, and I don't think you want to either. She'll still have two parents who love her, because I know you love her.'

'What are you saying, Mia?'

They were pulling up outside the *salon*. Mia put her hand on the door handle. 'I think it's best if we divorce. I'll obviously wait until you and Devilliers deem it a good time. But I want a divorce, Daniel. I want to have a chance at finding happiness, even if you don't. As you said yourself, I'm no pushover and I'm not swayed by money. So I'm not going to change my mind.'

Daniel watched Mia get out of the car and walk into the apartment. He couldn't move. He felt numb. He couldn't believe what she'd just said. She didn't mean it. She couldn't.

Love.

Having that responsibility for someone else's happiness made Daniel feel a blackness descending over him. The only person he'd ever loved had died. And that grief and toxicity had spread outwards, infecting everything. Love only brought pain, grief, abandonment.

They didn't need love. And after the launch tonight he would show Mia—convince her that what they had was enough.

A few hours later Mia was ready for the launch party. She hadn't even been aware of being got ready. She'd stood still as the team had worked around her, allowing her to feel hollowed out, which suited her fine. She didn't want to talk to anyone. She'd done enough talking today.

She was made up to resemble the way she looked in the campaign. Her hair was smoothed and slicked back, caught in a low ponytail. Her dress was strapless and black, down to her knee, with a slit up one thigh. So far, so simple—except that it was leather.

When Mia saw herself in it, her eyes almost fell out of her head. 'I can't wear this,' she whispered in shock. It clung to her body like an indecent second skin. It was pure...*sex*.

'*Madame*, it is...sublime.'

Mia shivered in spite of herself as a purely feminine thrill went through her.

The woman in charge of the jewellery brought over the necklace Mia was to wear tonight—a very stark and bold piece. A huge ruby set into a gold neckpiece that coiled around her neck and trailed down to sit just above her cleavage. It was eye-catching.

Mia took off her other jewellery: her engagement ring and wedding ring. She felt a pang, because she'd worn them for such a short time, and probably wouldn't be wearing them for much longer.

At that moment Daniel appeared in the doorway, in a black tuxedo. Every inch the sexy, suave billionaire. The shocked expression from earlier was gone. Now he looked impassive.

Her silly heart clenched. Had what she'd said made any impact or had her words almost literally rolled off his back?

* * *

The moment Daniel looked at Mia in that dress, the numbness encasing him since she'd stepped out of the car earlier was obliterated by pure electricity.

She looked like a sultry siren from a *film noir.* All sleek golden limbs, with her body shrink-wrapped into a dress that was pure sin. He wanted to tell the stylist to change the dress immediately—in this she would cause accidents, heart attacks. But they didn't have time. And he had approved the dress after all. Except in the picture on the mannequin it had looked positively benign.

He looked at Mia's face. She was watching him warily. What she'd said earlier had been so outrageous that he still wasn't entirely sure that she'd actually said it.

Paul the butler appeared. 'The car is ready downstairs.'

Daniel forced himself to focus. What Mia had said earlier was nonsense. They just needed to talk about it.

He led her out of the apartment. Her scent was fresh and light—at odds with the outfit— reminding him of who she really was. Of her contradictions.

Odile and Lexi were waiting to say goodbye in the foyer and Odile said, 'Wow, Mia…you look amazing.'

Lexi copied Odile. 'Wow… Mama…'mazing.'

Mia laughed and hugged Odile and Lexi. Then Lexi put her arms out towards Daniel. He lifted her up, inhaling her sweet scent. She planted a kiss on his cheek.

His chest felt tight. *'Merci, mignonne.'*

He handed her back to Odile, and they left.

There was silence in the car as it wound its way

from Place Vendôme to the venue. Daniel could see the toned length of Mia's thigh. She was looking away, out of the window. He wanted to turn her face to him, make her look at him. Cover her mouth with his.

It suddenly occurred to him, then, that in the past week, in spite of the intensity of their lovemaking, she hadn't kissed him on the mouth once. Everywhere but the mouth. As if she was denying him something that some considered more intimate than actual intercourse. In fact she hadn't even kissed him on the mouth on their wedding night.

No. Not possible. He was losing it. Imagining it.

What she'd said earlier...it was scrambling his brain.

An ache built in his chest, but he ignored it. They pulled up outside the venue and Daniel got out and went around to help Mia out of the car. He had to clench his jaw to keep his body under control as she uncoiled her tall body in that dress.

As soon as they saw her, the paparazzi went wild.

Now they knew her name.

'Mia, Mia! Over here! Mia!'

Daniel stood to the side, for once out of the limelight and not minding it one bit. Mia posed with professional ease, but he could see that she was trembling lightly.

He went over and took her hand, saying to the photographers, *'Ça suffit.'* Enough.

He led her to the entrance. Her hand was tight around his.

He looked down at her. 'Okay?'

She looked up and nodded. 'I'm just not used to this level of attention.'

Daniel put his thumb and forefinger to her chin and tipped it up. He bent down to press his mouth against hers, but at the last second she turned her head, denying him her lips.

Something dark spiralled in Daniel's gut as his kiss landed on her cheek.

He hadn't been imagining it.

As soon as they walked into the venue a hush fell over the crowd. Daniel felt a surge of protectiveness. He kept hold of Mia's hand, but after a while her death grip loosened and she let go. And at one point she turned to him and said, 'I'm okay now. You can do whatever you have to do.'

Daniel saw that she was with Adele, the photographer. He said, 'I have to make a speech, but we can go after that.'

Mia nodded and her gaze slid away from his.

They got separated by the crowd.

He kept looking for her over the heads of everyone else, but only caught glimpses here and there. This was a pinnacle moment for him and the business, and yet he couldn't focus on it.

Someone touched his arm and he almost snarled at them to leave him alone. It was his chief assistant.

'Okay, boss?'

Daniel forced himself to relax. 'Fine.'

'It's time for your speech.'

His speech. Damn. It was the last thing he felt like doing now.

He said to Pascal, 'Can you find Mia and stay with her? Make sure she's okay?'

'Of course.'

Daniel made his way to the dais and was introduced by one of France's best-loved actresses, who had been a brand ambassador for Devilliers for a long time. She graciously mentioned that Mia was part of a new generation of ambassadors and wished her well.

Daniel still couldn't see Mia in the crowd, but finally caught sight of her. She was standing with Pascal and Adele. Relief flooded his belly. He launched into his speech, not having to check his notes because he'd been preparing for this a long time.

He mentioned Mia too, and thanked her for elevating the campaign beyond the ordinary and into something extraordinary. He could see her blush from where he stood, as everyone clapped and congratulated her.

That ache resurfaced, and absently he put a hand to his chest as he made his closing remarks. When he looked to where Mia had been standing just moments ago, though, she was no longer there. He kept speaking on autopilot as he searched for her. And then he saw her, slipping out of an exit, shoulders bare.

He stumbled over his words. Had to stop, look at his notes.

Where was she going?

Eventually he finished his speech and there was deafening applause, but all Daniel cared about was finding Mia. He kept getting stopped by people. And she was nowhere to be seen. The pictures from the campaign were on the walls all around the room, like a gallery exhibit, and everywhere he looked, Mia's face stared back seductively. Mockingly.

'I want a divorce, Daniel. I want to have a chance at finding happiness...'

Finally, *finally*, he got to the exit and saw his driver. He went over. 'Have you seen Mia?'

'I just dropped her home, sir, and came back to wait for you.'

Daniel looked behind him and saw the glittering crowd. He knew he had to go back. *Should* go back.

But he got into the car instead.

CHAPTER ELEVEN

MIA WINCED AS she contorted herself again in front of the mirror in the dressing room. It was no good. She needed help to get out of the dress but she'd sent Odile home when she'd arrived back a short time before, and she wasn't about to scandalise Paul, so she would have to wait.

She'd done her best to comb the gel out of her hair, but washing it would have to wait too. At least it didn't feel as if it was shrink-wrapped to her head any more.

She felt bad about leaving the party early, but—

She heard a noise and looked up. Daniel stood in the doorway, looking a little wild-eyed. 'You're here,' he said.

Mia felt guilty. 'Sorry. I just… It all got a bit overwhelming. I went out to get some air and saw the driver. I asked him to bring me home. I sent you a text.'

Daniel pulled out his phone as if he'd never seen it before.

Mia said, 'You should go back. I'm sorry for pulling you away.'

Daniel put his phone back and shook his head as

he tugged his bowtie loose. 'The speech is done. No one will notice I'm gone at this stage.'

Mia doubted that very much. 'You should go back,' she repeated. 'It's a big night.'

He said, 'I'll go back if you come with me.'

Mia pointed to her undone hair. And then her bare feet. 'Like this? I don't think your board would approve of the *"before"* version of the model in their campaign.'

Daniel walked towards Mia. 'I think the "before" version is better.'

She swallowed. 'Daniel, I'm serious. You should be there.'

He stopped just inches away. Mia had to look up.

He said, 'I'm perfectly happy here.'

There was a volatile energy coming off Daniel that Mia had never noticed before. He was always so in control. Even when he lost control. But this connected with something equally volatile in her. The desperation that had led her to say what she had earlier. And she still didn't know what Daniel thought about it.

'Daniel, we should talk…about what I said…'

But his gaze was dropping down over her body in the leather dress. Lingering on her breasts, belly, hips. Legs. Back up. Eyes glittering.

'I don't think I can talk while you're wearing that dress.'

Mia turned around, presenting him with her back. 'Then can you help me get out of it, please? So we can talk. I can't undo it myself.'

She pulled her hair over one shoulder. She hated

herself for it, but when Daniel moved close behind her she wasn't thinking much about talking either.

Familiar tension coiled in her gut as she waited to feel his fingers on the zip. But instead his hands came to her shoulders. Breath feathered over her and she felt his mouth touch her skin, pressing kisses along her upper back.

'Daniel...' she said weakly, her legs turning to rubber.

'Do you want me to stop?'

Yes, Mia said inwardly, because she knew that after what she'd said today she had no defences left. But the temptation was too much. She needed this. Needed it like a lifeforce. And after this she might never experience it again.

She turned around, eyes locking on Daniel's mouth. She'd denied herself that mouth on hers in some misguided idea that it would be easier to *have sex* than *make love*. It hadn't worked.

'No, damn you,' she said now. 'I don't want you to stop.'

She reached up and wrapped her arms around his neck and kissed him, almost sobbing with relief when, after a moment's hesitation, he kissed her back. Mouths open. Tongues tangling. Why had she denied herself this?

Because it's going to shatter your heart into a million pieces when you leave...

Mia shoved the voice down deep. Not now.

Daniel hauled her up against his body and carried her over to a wide chair in the dressing room, sitting down and taking her with him.

'Put your legs either side of mine.'

Mia looked down at the unforgiving dress. 'I don't think I—'

There was a sound of material ripping and Mia saw that Daniel had ripped the slit in the dress so that it reached her hip. She looked at him, and he looked like the devil incarnate. Her skin went on fire.

He said, 'Now try.'

She put her thighs either side of his, and he reached around her back to pull the zip down. She shivered as the dress loosened around her breasts and Daniel pulled at the bodice, freeing her breasts. He cupped them, thumbs finding her nipples and stroking them to hard points.

Mia couldn't think straight. Her hands were on the back of the chair behind Daniel's head, and then her own head fell back when Daniel leant forward and put his mouth on one breast and then the other, suckling her flesh until she was panting and moving against him, seeking a deeper connection.

He put his hands on her hips. 'Come up for me, *chérie.*'

Mia came up on her knees. Heard Daniel undo his belt and trousers. Heard the ripping of a foil packet. And then his hands were on her hips again and he was bringing her down slowly onto his shaft.

It was exquisite torture as he slowly urged her up and down, lubricating his body with her own, her muscles massaging his length until they were both half crazed. Daniel held her still so that he could dictate the pace, and he surged up into her body over and over again, putting his mouth on her breast and sucking her nipple so hard that she had nowhere to go except hurtling over the edge.

For long moments they stayed in that embrace. Daniel's head on Mia's breast, her head buried in his neck, her thighs trembling in the aftermath.

The following morning when Daniel woke he noticed the utter stillness. He felt cold. He'd had dreams… awful dreams. Dreams of being in a large venue, seeing glimpses of Mia, but then she'd disappear again. Round and round he went, searching for her endlessly…

Last night…

The frantic sex came back to him in snatches. Ripping Mia's dress to her hip. Her breasts falling free of the restrictive leather. The desperation that had fuelled them to that explosive climax.

Eventually she'd extricated herself and gone. Daniel had presumed to change, freshen up. He'd waited for her. But she hadn't come back. The door to the nursery had been closed and, aware of Lexi, he hadn't wanted to disturb her.

He'd taken a shower and come into his bedroom, half expecting—*hoping*—that she might be in his bed. But it had been empty.

He remembered the way she'd looked when she'd said, *'No, damn you, I don't want you to stop.'* As if she'd wanted him but resented it.

Daniel went even colder now. She'd whispered something into his neck before she'd left him sitting on that chair in a stupor. He'd heard it at the time, but he'd ignored it. Now it came back.

She'd said, very clearly, 'This doesn't change anything.'

Daniel jack-knifed up to sit in the bed. The stillness in the apartment seemed to permeate his bones.

She was gone.

He got up, pulling on sweats. Lexi's bedroom door was open. The bed was made. Lexi's cot empty. No unintelligible chatter signalled her presence.

Paul wasn't even here. No one was here.

Daniel had a flashback to walking around the chateau where he'd grown up. He'd woken up one day to find the chateau empty. Totally empty. It had been shortly after Delphine's death. Finally, that evening, his father had returned from Paris to find Daniel curled up in the corner of his bedroom, practically catatonic with fear and bewilderment.

He'd believed he'd been abandoned because he'd been responsible for Delphine's death.

'What's wrong with you, boy?'

Daniel had looked up and known he should be feeling relief that his father was there, but all he'd felt was cold.

'Where did everyone go?' he'd asked.

His father had cursed. 'You were left here today?'

Daniel had nodded.

'Your mother was supposed to take you with her to the South of France,' his father had spat out. 'The staff were given the day off to go to a fête in the village.'

There had been no apology or acknowledgement of the fact that he'd been abandoned. He'd just spent the rest of that week going into the *salon* with his irritated father. And when his mother had returned from the South of France she hadn't said a thing.

Daniel thought of Lexi and subjecting her to a similar experience. It made him feel physically ill and gave him a wholly new perspective on the cruelty of his parents.

He rubbed at his chest.

He knew one thing above everything else. Mia couldn't leave him. And he had to tell her that.

He forced himself to be rational. She couldn't be far. She wouldn't have just left so suddenly. He needed to talk to her. To try and explain something he couldn't even explain to himself.

Mia watched Lexi throw morsels of bread to the ducks. She felt numb. She'd made herself feel numb to stop images from last night running in her head. Last night had just proved that she wasn't strong enough to love Daniel and stay with him.

Lexi started toddling towards the playground. Mia took her hand.

'Mia!'

She stopped, turned around. Daniel was behind her, looking very dishevelled. A loose shirt over jeans. Shoes with no socks. No coat. She'd never seen him like this.

'Daniel?'

'I need to talk to you.'

Mia saw Odile, not far behind Daniel. 'What's Odile doing here? Has something happened? You're scaring me.'

He shook his head. 'No, nothing is wrong. I just need Odile to watch Lexi so we can talk.'

Bemused, Mia greeted Odile and handed over Lexi's bag and stroller. Odile was discreet enough to say, 'Don't worry. I'll stay with her until I hear from you.'

Lexi trotted off happily with Odile to the playground. Mia turned to Daniel. Even now she was aware of the looks he drew. Mainly because he looked as if he'd literally just tumbled out of bed. She wanted to snarl at all the women that he was *hers*. But he wasn't. Not really.

'What is it, Daniel?'

He indicated a bench. 'Sit with me for a minute?'

They sat down.

Daniel turned to Mia and she tried to channel every bit of inner strength she had to withstand his proximity and his effect on her.

'I don't want you to leave, Mia.'

'Look, Daniel, I really, really wanted to make this work—especially for Lexi's sake. And maybe it would if I didn't feel the way I do... But it'll kill me in the end, knowing you don't feel the same way.'

'But that's it... I do... I mean, I think I do. Or that I can.'

Mia felt sick. 'I think I'd prefer it if you pretended you were in love with me, Daniel. But you don't even know...'

Mia stood up and started walking. This was humiliating. Daniel was so desperate for her to stay that he was clearly doing his best to conjure up some sort of emotion to persuade her.

'Mia, wait.'

She stopped. Daniel came alongside her.

'I'm not making sense, I know. I need to show you something that might help you understand...will you come with me?'

Mia wanted to say no, but she was more intrigued than she liked to admit, so she said a grudging, 'Fine.'

When they got to Place Vendôme there was a car she hadn't seen before out front—a low-slung sports car. Daniel opened the passenger door.

She hesitated. 'Where are we going?'

'For a drive. It's about an hour—is that okay?'

Mia shrugged. 'Do I have a choice?'

'Of course you do, but I'd like you to give me this chance.'

Dammit, that flicker of hope was back.

Mia got into the car. It was a luxurious cocoon. Daniel put on some music. They were soon out of the city and speeding along the motorway before turning off and taking country roads.

Mia tried not to think about what Daniel had up his sleeve to convince her to stay. She was determined not to be swayed. He didn't even know how he felt about her. It was insulting!

At about the hour mark they passed through a post-card-pretty village, and on the other side followed a high stone wall for about ten minutes, before Daniel turned into an opening where there were huge gates. She saw his hands tense on the wheel as he waited for a security guard to open the gates and let them in.

Daniel's tension was palpable now. His jaw was tight. Mia felt uneasy. 'Where are we?'

'The Devilliers chateau.'

Where Delphine had died. Where he'd grown up.

His words came back to her: *'My background broke me'*.

Mia said nothing as they made their winding way up a seemingly endless drive. And then suddenly the chateau appeared around a bend. Mia sucked in a breath. This was not your quintessential pretty French chateau. This was something out of a gothic nightmare. Forbidding grey stone. Spiky ramparts. Small windows. It looked cold and oppressive.

Daniel parked in the front courtyard and got out, opening Mia's door and helping her out too. She didn't want to let go of his hand but had to. She was here to break with him, not cling to him.

He went up the steps and the door opened as he approached. A dour-looking man said, 'Welcome, Mr Devilliers, we weren't expecting you.'

'No,' he said, sounding grim. 'It's fine, we won't be here long.'

Mia smiled at the older man, but he stared at her as if she was a ghost. She really didn't like this place. It was as cold and forbidding inside as out.

The man walked away, and Daniel waited till he was gone. Then he looked at Mia. 'I really would prefer if you hadn't had to see this place, but it's the only way I know how to show you…'

Show me what? she wanted to ask.

But instead she just let him lead her from room to room. He pointed out Delphine's room, untouched from the day she'd died. Mia's heart broke to see the toys and books.

Daniel told Mia about the day he'd found himself alone, with no idea where everyone was. Ice crept into her blood at the thought of him as a small boy, grief-struck, alone in this inhospitable place.

And eventually he took her outside to the back, where the manicured gardens looked frozen in time. The sun was shining but she still felt cold.

Daniel led her around the side of the chateau, to an area of ground that looked slightly different from the rest. She recognised the shape.

'This was the pool, wasn't it?'

Daniel nodded.

'You had it filled in?'

'My mother did.'

'Oh, Daniel…' Mia couldn't stop the emotion.

He didn't look at her as he said, 'I know rationally that it wasn't my fault she died. As you pointed out, I was only nine. But it's embedded on my soul in a way I can't seem to erase. I loved Delphine so much…she was the only joy in my life, and me in hers. I prob-ably would have survived this place quite well if she had lived. Our parents' neglect made us even closer. But when she died, I felt that somehow I'd caused it by needing her too much. That I didn't deserve to have her in my life. Then my mother's reaction…my father's lack of emotion…compounded my guilt.'

He turned to her then. He looked so tortured that Mia's heart broke all over again.

'But I know that I have to let it go, or I'll never be

free to trust that something good can come of needing you and Lexi in my life. To trust that needing you won't somehow…destroy you. I didn't want to bring you here to tell you all of this,' he continued, 'but I had to. Because it's the only way I know to show you what's in here…' he put a hand over his heart '…and to try and tell you how you make me feel.'

Mia took Daniel's hands, her heart speeding up a little. 'How *do* I make you feel?'

'When I saw you walk out of the party yesterday evening I couldn't concentrate. I had to find you. The thought of you and Lexi…going…of not seeing you every day…of not having you in my bed, in my life… it makes my chest physically hurt. I feel like I can't breathe.'

He said, 'I know now that's love, Mia. I love you and Lexi. I loved you from the minute I saw you, but I had no capacity to recognise it. When you said you were pregnant… I felt sheer terror. The thought of bringing a child into the world, when all I knew was abandonment and the pain of grief… I didn't see how I wouldn't pass that on. That's why I said what I said that day.'

Mia kept silent. Letting him find his words.

'But then you came back…with Lexi…and I couldn't hide from the demons. I had to let you in. I thought I could do that and somehow stay removed from how you made me feel. The reason I wanted to marry you so quickly was because I knew that if you had time to think about it you'd realise it was too much of a sacrifice. Not because I cared about what people thought. But I'm terrified that loving you will somehow harm you and Lexi.'

He took his hands out of hers. Mia's heart broke in two. The tone in Daniel's voice was the opposite of self-pity. He really believed what he'd said. She could see how damaging this place had been.

Mia said, 'I'm glad you brought me here.'

'You are?'

She nodded. 'You're right. I wouldn't have understood. But now I do. And there's one thing I know.'

'What?'

Mia shuddered lightly. 'Lexi is never coming here.'

Daniel's mouth thinned. 'No way.'

Mia took his hands again. 'And neither are we, coming back here—ever. Because we're going to sell it.'

A wary look came over his face. 'We?'

She nodded. Saw something very fragile make his eyes bright.

'But it's been in the family for centuries…'

Mia shrugged. 'So what?'

The ghost of a smile touched Daniel's mouth. 'Typical American. No appreciation of culture.'

Mia shook her head, joy bubbling up from deep inside her. 'Nope. We'll buy another chateau. A pink one.'

Daniel looked horrified. 'Pink?'

Mia cocked her head on one side. 'Yes. Pink. I've always thought they're so pretty.'

Daniel's expression became serious. Wary again. 'Mia, are you saying you'll stay?'

She moved closer and stretched up, pressing a kiss against Daniel's mouth. A sweet kiss. A benediction.

'If you'll have me. And Lexi.'

She felt the shudder of emotion that ran through Daniel. He gathered her close.

'If I have any chance in this world, it's with you and Lexi. And even though the thought of loving you and causing any harm to come to you and Lexi terrifies me, the thought of letting you go terrifies me more. Is that selfish?'

Mia kissed him again. 'No, my love, it's supremely human. But loving us can't possibly harm us. I can't guarantee that nothing bad will happen, but I can guarantee that no matter what we'll be together, and together we can face anything.'

Daniel cupped her face and said fervently, 'Don't ever stop kissing me, Mia.'

'Never, my love.'

EPILOGUE

Costa Rica

MIA WALKED DOWN through the trees to the beach and sat down on the seat that Daniel had had made, set in the shade. She sat there and adjusted the baby, so that she could feed him under the strategically placed muslin cloth. Not that there was anyone to see her breastfeed. It was off-season, and the beach was practically empty.

They'd exchanged their vows again here, about three years ago, in a beautiful dawn ceremony, with Lexi bearing the ring that Mia now wore on her right hand. A simple band of gold on one side, and inlaid with diamonds on the other. An eternity ring.

She was slowly but surely accruing more jewellery—which was only befitting the wife of one of the world's most renowned jewellers.

She smiled as she took in the scene before her. Daniel was standing in the sea, with five-year-old Lexi in his arms. She was squealing with delight every time he dunked her under the water and lifted her up again.

'Again, Papa, *again*!'

He obliged. Indefatigable when it came to his beloved daughter, catering to her every whim without ever spoiling her. They were as thick as thieves, and it gave Mia such bittersweet joy to see their bond, because now she had an even truer sense of what she'd missed out on.

And now their little family was growing, with Dominic—Dom for short. They'd waited a while to have another baby, giving Lexi time to get used to Daniel, and time for them all to get used to being in a family. A *real* family.

The baby suckled contentedly at Mia's breast. The birth had been incredibly emotional, because seeing Daniel's joy had compounded her guilt that he'd missed Lexi's birth. But that night after the birth, as he'd held Dom and sat by Mia's bed, Daniel had taken her hand and kissed it, and then he had shaken his head, intuiting her distress.

'Stop it, *mon amour*. I'm as responsible as you for what happened and how it happened. More so. We have so much to be grateful for. I love you, and you've made me the happiest man in the world. I can't wait to spend the rest of my life with you and our children. No going back—only forward. I love you.'

Mia had cried, exhausted and emotional and full of love, and Daniel had kissed her tears away, healing the past, anointing the future.

As if sensing her presence, Daniel looked over and saw her. He pointed over to them and Lexi squealed.

'Mama and Dommy!'

Daniel strode out of the water, Lexi held high in his

arms, her dark hair slicked back with water, exposing her pretty face.

In the past few years Daniel had not only overcome his demons about his sister's death and his fear of the water, he had gone a step further by learning how to scuba dive. Now he was never out of the water, and it made Mia stupidly emotional every time she saw it or swam with him. Although admittedly, if they were in the water together, inevitably not much swimming happened…

'Thinking lusty thoughts again?' he asked when they came close, with a familiar gleam in his eye.

'What's lusty, Papa?' Lexi piped up as she scrambled down from Daniel's arms to go and sit beside Mia and check up on her beloved baby brother.

Mia's cheeks burned betrayingly and she scowled at Daniel, who of course knew exactly what she was thinking. He sat down on the bench beside her, moving Lexi to his lap.

Lexi asked, 'Can I hold Dommy, Mama?'

Dom was already pulling away from her breast, hearing his sister's voice. Mia gave up for now. Plenty of time to feed later. She adjusted her clothes, winded Dom briefly, and then handed him carefully to Lexi, who took him into her arms with a deeply furrowed brow, handling him as if he was a fragile piece of glass.

'That's it, *cherie*, very good,' Daniel said encouragingly, careful to support Lexi in holding the baby without making it too obvious.

At that moment an older couple who had been walking down the beach passed by, hand in hand. They looked at Daniel and Mia and their family and smiled indulgently, saying, *'Pura vida.'* The Costa Rican saying that encapsulated everything from *Hello!* To *Life is good!* To its most simple translation *Pure life!* or *Simple life!*

Good life.

Mia smiled and looked at Daniel. Understanding passed between them.

What they had was so much more than a pure or simple life. They had the perfect life. And a family full of love. And a deep and intense understanding that love was always deserved. For ever.

And, yes, they'd sold the dark and scary chateau and bought a pink one...covered in ivy and filled it full of happiness and love.

* * * * *

If you were caught up in
Bound by Her Shocking Secret
you'll love these other stories by Abby Green!

The Greek's Unknown Bride
The Maid's Best Kept Secret
The Innocent Behind the Scandal
Bride Behind the Desert Veil
The Flaw in His Red-Hot Revenge

Available now!

WE HOPE YOU ENJOYED
THIS BOOK FROM
⟨H⟩ HARLEQUIN
PRESENTS

Escape to exotic locations where passion knows no bounds.

Welcome to the glamorous lives of royals and billionaires, where passion knows no bounds. Be swept into a world of luxury, wealth and exotic locations.

8 NEW BOOKS AVAILABLE EVERY MONTH!

#3965 A CONTRACT FOR HIS RUNAWAY BRIDE
The Scandalous Campbell Sisters
by Melanie Milburne
Elodie needs billion-dollar backing to make a success of her fashion brand. As if pitching to a billionaire wasn't hard enough, Lincoln Lancaster is her ex-fiancé! He'll help her, but his deal has one condition: she'll finally meet him at the altar...

#3966 RECLAIMED FOR HIS ROYAL BED
by Maya Blake
Having tracked Delphine down, King Lucca can finally lay his family's scandalous past to rest...if she agrees to play the golden couple in public. And once again set alight by his touch, will Delphine reveal the explosive reason why she left?

#3967 THE INNOCENT'S PROTECTOR IN PARADISE
by Annie West
Tycoon Niall is the only person Lola can turn to when her life is threatened. He immediately offers her a hiding place—his private Gold Coast retreat! He's utterly off-limits, but their fierce desire incinerates any resistance...

#3968 THE BILLIONAIRE WITHOUT RULES
Lost Sons of Argentina
by Lucy King
Billionaire Max plays by his own rules, but there's one person that stands between him and the truth of his birth: tantalizingly tenacious private investigator Alex. And she's demanding they do things her way!

YOU CAN FIND MORE INFORMATION ON UPCOMING HARLEQUIN TITLES, FREE EXCERPTS AND MORE AT HARLEQUIN.COM.

HPCNMRB1121

SPECIAL EXCERPT FROM

(H) HARLEQUIN

PRESENTS

*Elodie needs billion-dollar backing to make a success
of her fashion brand. As if pitching to a billionaire
wasn't hard enough, Lincoln Lancaster is her ex-fiancé!
He'll help her, but his deal has one condition: she'll
finally meet him at the altar...*

*Read on for a sneak preview of debut author
Melanie Milburne's next story for Harlequin Presents,*
A Contract for His Runaway Bride.

"Could you give me an update on when Mr. Smith will be available?"

The receptionist's answering smile was polite but formal. "I apologize for the delay. He'll be with you shortly."

"Look, my appointment was—"

"I understand, Ms Campbell. But he's a very busy man. He's made a special gap in his schedule for you. He's not usually so accommodating. You must've made a big impression on him."

"I haven't even met him. All I know is I was instructed to be here close to thirty minutes ago for a meeting with a Mr. Smith to discuss finance. I've been given no other details."

The receptionist glanced at the intercom console, where a small green light was flashing. She looked up again at Elodie with the same polite smile. "Thank you for being so patient. Mr.…erm… Smith will see you now. Please go through. It's the third door on the right. The corner office."

The corner office boded well—that meant he was the head honcho. The big bucks began and stopped with him. Elodie came to the door and took a deep, calming breath, but it did nothing to settle the frenzy of switchblades in her stomach. She gave the door a quick rap with her knuckles. *Please, please, please let me be successful this time.*

"Come."

Her hand paused on the doorknob, her mind whirling in ice-cold panic. Something about the deep timbre of that voice sent a shiver scuttling over her scalp like a small claw-footed creature. How could this Mr. Smith sound so like her ex-fiancé? Scarily alike. She turned the doorknob and pushed the door open, her gaze immediately fixing on the tall dark-haired man behind the large desk.

"You?" Elodie gasped, heat flooding into her cheeks and other places in her body she didn't want to think about right now.

Lincoln Lancaster rose from his chair with leonine grace, his expression set in its customary cynical lines—the arch of one ink-black brow over his intelligent blue-green gaze, the tilt of his sensual mouth that was not quite a smile. His black hair was brushed back from his high forehead in loose waves that looked like they had last been combed by his fingers. He was dressed in a three-piece suit that hugged his athletic frame, emphasizing the broadness of his shoulders, the taut trimness of his chest, flat abdomen and lean hips. He was the epitome of successful a man in his prime. Potent, powerful, persuasive. He got what he wanted, when he wanted, how he wanted.

"You're looking good, Elodie." His voice rolled over her as smoothly and lazily as his gaze, the deep, sexy rumble so familiar it brought up a host of memories she had fought for seven years to erase. Memories in her flesh that were triggered by being in his presence. Erotic memories that made her hyperaware of his every breath, his every glance, his every movement.

Don't miss
A Contract for His Runaway Bride,
available December 2021 wherever
Harlequin Presents books and ebooks are sold.

Harlequin.com